PRAISE FOR DOROTHY NELSON

"For women who have experienced the intimidation of a
city at night, and learned where the power in society rests,
this book will find a friend."
—*Workers Life*

"*In Night's City* is a promising investigation of this dark realm of
the complexity of family emotion, a realm in which the shapes of
ordinary life assume strange, hallucinatory appearances."
—*Irish Press*

"One of the better pieces of fiction that I've read over the last
while. . . . The characters live and you live through them."
—*Image Magazine*

"A highly original debut."
—*Sunday Independent*

ALSO BY DOROTHY NELSON

Tar and Feathers

DOROTHY NELSON

IN NIGHT'S CITY

DALKEY ARCHIVE PRESS
NORMAL · LONDON

First U.S. edition, 2006

Library of Congress Cataloging-in-Publication Data available.
ISBN: 1-56478-418-5

Partially funded by grants from the National Endowment for the Arts,
a federal agency, and the Illinois Arts Council, a state agency.

Dalkey Archive Press is a nonprofit organization whose mission is
to promote international cultural understanding and provide
a forum for dialogue for the literary arts.

www.dalkeyarchive.com

Printed on permanent/durable acid-free paper, bound in the United States of
America, and distributed throughout North America and Europe.

Chapter 1

SARA – FEBRUARY 1970

"Tickle me the way you tickle my Mammy," I said. I climbed up on the bed and he smiled down. The colours were runnin' down his face like a river. Bright splashing colours. "Go on tickle me," I said. An' he tickled my belly with his colours. "I have a secret," I said. "Mammy says I've to tell no-one 'specially not you." "Are you goin' to tell me it?" he said. "Tickle me again an' I'll tell," I said. "It's a big secret." "I swear I won't tell anybody," he said laughin'. "Let me in beside you first," I said. I got in under the covers where it was soft. "Well then," he said. "What's the big secret?" "Me an' Mammy went down the town an' we turned a road an' then another road. We saw you sittin' in the car with a lady an' Mammy hurt my arm an' said I wasn't to tell no-one. 'Specially not you. I see your colours Daddy," I said. "I see them." He laughed down an' all the colours grew bright an' came runnin' down his face. "Say how old I am, say?" I said. "You're three!" he said, an' he tickled me. "No I'm not. Three is a baby. I'm four now. Say it Daddy. Say how old I am." "Three-and-a-half," he said. The laughin' came closer. "I'm not three-and-a-half. I just told you, I'm four now." He tickled me again an' I was laughin' into his colours. Then it was dark. I felt the Dark touchin' me funny an' I was cryin' so Maggie came an' he touched Maggie funny not me. Not me. Not me.

The Big Dark was grindin' the Little Dark's bones to smithereens. Then the bones were a white dust an' the dust began to whirl an' fall on my bed. It came higher an' higher until I was sucked down under it an' I couldn't breathe.

He was looking down on me and then he pulled the blankets off me an' touched me funny. Mammy came in an' I thought "It'll be all right now. It'll be all right." It was dark but she didn't turn the light on. She stood beside my pillow an' looked at him doin' the funny things. Her eyes were sort of glintin' and she looked real cold. I went to say "Mammy stop him hurtin' me," but she wasn't mindin' me. She was in the faraway place watchin' him doin' the funny things so I pretended I wasn't there. Then he went downstairs and she went into the toilet. When she came back she switched the light on an' I started to cry. "Look," I said. "Look is that red blood on the sheets? Is it Mammy?" She came over an' pulled the covers up and told me to lie down. "Go to sleep now," she said. "You had a bad dream." "It wasn't a dream, Mammy," I said. "It was real." She bent down over me. "It was a dream. Now go to sleep." "It wasn't Mammy," I cried. "Say it wasn't. Look." I pushed the covers down and showed her the red blood. "Look at that," I said. "It was a dream," she said. "Now lie down and go to sleep." "It wasn't, Mammy. Say it wasn't. Say it was real." When she was gone I switched the light on again to look at the blood. "Look at it, Maggie," I said. "She said it was a dream but it wasn't. It was real." Maggie came to have a look an' she started laughin' mad an' then I laughed too. I kept pointin' at the red blood and laughin' my head off.

Anne walked up the stairs ahead of me. I could see the sun streaming in through the window in the middle of the stairway. When she stepped into the stream of light it shone on her fuzzy hair an' I could see the nits climbin' in through the knots an' tangles.

"Anne!" I called up after her. She turned around in the sun. "Can they fly?" I asked.

"What did you say, Sara Kavanagh?"

"Them nits," I said, pointing with my finger. "Can they

fly? You're not to sit beside me anymore if they can."

"There's no nits in my hair, you," she said. An' she ran on ahead of me up the stairs. The way she said that stopped me, as if she knew as well as I did but she was saying "No" 'cause if you say "No" it means they're not there.

She sat beside me as usual an' my eyes kept strayin' over to the tangles. When the sun wasn't shinin' you couldn't see but I kept scratchin' my head 'cause maybe they could an' she just wouldn't say. She bent over her copybook like she always did when she didn't know the answers. I couldn't stand to see the way she huddled over her book as if she was terrified, with her eyes dartin' around to see if everyone else was writing. So I wrote the answers down on a piece of paper as best I could and passed them over. She set the paper on her lap under the desk and wrote them into her book. It was a funny thing. She hardly ever spoke a word. She just came an' went like a piece of dust that didn't want to be seen. She was standin' by the window leanin' on the brush and lookin' out at the sky. The soft was there. I could see the blue an' pink soft like little lappin' waves an' then the grey came an' I shivered in the cold. The grey kept hopping in over the pink and blue washin' them away like the winter rain washin' the colours off the face of the world. "You all right, Mammy?" I asked. But she couldn't hear me so I tried to slide in to where the pink an' blue was but the grey kept gettin' in the way an' I couldn't find her.

I could see them again in the sun when she walked up the stairs. Millions crawlin' around in her hair like it was a playground.

"Hey you, Anne," I said. "Wait for me." She pressed in against the wall to let the other girls go by.

"Just tell me," I said. "Say, 'Yes' or 'No'. Can they fly?"

Her face squeezed up real tight like a cryin' face.

"They're not there," she said. "Leave me alone you."

"Doesn't your mother wash your hair?"

"I haven't got a mother."

" 'Course you have. Everyone has a mother."

"No I haven't. She's dead." She started to walk ahead of me but I ran to catch up.

"When'd she die then?"

"I don't know. A long time ago," she said.

"Mothers don't die. I never heard of anyone's mother dead before."

She sat me up on her lap an' held me against her cardigan. It smelled of her.

"I haven't got nits," she said. "I haven't." And she turned an' ran back down the stairs into the toilets.

She was a jewel. Anne was a jewel. I could see the sun shinin' on her hair an' the nits sparkled in the sun. "They can't fly because they are jewels," I said. Anne O'Sullivan has no mother, I wrote in my head, she has jewels but they can't fly.

When Ma told me he was dead I didn't think 'Father you are' but, 'Sweat and breath you are'. Not 'Father you are' but, 'Sweat and breath mingling with my own you are'.

"Pull yourself together now," she said. When I looked around she was holding her hands to her head as if she was going to split down the middle at any second.

I went up to the toilet and sat on the edge of the bath. I had wanted him to die slow. He would be lying in bed under the white starched sheets. A face without a body. And the wheeze coming up his lungs filling that room and echoing from wall to wall. His large hands would reach out from under the bedclothes to touch mine. The tips of his fingers against the palms of my hands. The tears spurting out of his eyes and I saying, 'Too late. Too late. Let your tears turn to blood and drip down the walls and ceiling of this room. Bloody the four feet space between your bed and mine for the past twenty years.'

"Stop your dreaming," Maggie says chuckling.

"Go away, Maggie. You haven't stopped laughing since she told me. They'll hear you and think it's me."

"Whose mouth then?" she asks. "Whose mouth?" I stood up and looked in the mirror over the bath and saw the way my mouth was, curled up in a sneer and the chuckling coming from it. I clenched my lips real tight together so nothing could come out. She was quiet for a while and then she says, "Just you remember I'll be right here watching and waiting to see if you cry over that son-of-a-bitch."

But I couldn't cry because she was rising up so fast inside me and she wouldn't quieten down. I was afraid she might say something out of turn and I wouldn't be able to stop it coming. Maggie laughing because the man was dead. Man of the father. Not father you are but sweat and breath you are.

I washed my face with the end of the towel and then dried it. I looked in the mirror again and behind my eyes I could see her chuckling away to herself. I opened the door and went on down to the kitchen.

Willy leans back in his chair. The front legs rise up as he balances the weight of his body on the hind legs. The legs wobble from side to side as if they're about to give from under him but he manoeuvres them slowly back to the floor without letting them slip.

"I don't know what made me come on holidays this time of the year," he says. "I was plannin' on July. It was an impulse. Maybe I knew." His eyes move about the kitchen as he talks.

"You've changed the wallpaper then?"

"Yes," Ma says. "Last summer we got Pa Curran in to strip down the walls properly. Your Father wasn't able for it. It's the grease from the cooker makes it so dirty looking."

Ma has no taste. I remember when Pa Curran put the paper up I asked her why she didn't get a plain paper instead of gaudy flowers. "It'd make the room look bigger," I said.

"Are you complainin'?" she snapped. "Is this house not good enough for you now?"

"All I meant was . . . ."

"I know what you meant," she said. "I happen to like gaudy wallpaper as you call it."

Did you ever laugh? Did you ever once crack your face laughin'?

"I'll make a pot of tea," she says. "It'll calm us down."

"I can't believe it," says Willy. "It's all happened so fast. He was stretched out on the floor stiff as ice. Must have been a good two hours before we came in."

"Stop thinkin' about it," Ma says. "It'll do no good. Get out the cups. Joseph, get another chair from the sitting-room."

"Did you ever think about dyin'?" I asked him. He looked up over the rim of the paper. His eyes singing Sara, Sara.

"What makes you ask that? Do I look like I'm dying?" he said laughing over at me. "Can't wait to get rid of me, is that it then?"

"I was just wondering," I said. "Would you be afraid?" He looked up again. His eyes bright singing Sara, Sara.

"I suppose if I thought about it I would," he said, folding the paper and putting it on the back of the chair. "But I don't think about it. When you get to my age you won't either."

"I'll never be your age. You're an oul man now."

"Is that right," he said, leaning one arm on the table.

His eyes teasing me with the singing. The field was dizzy in my head. All the colours of the carnival wheeling down my mind where he was sitting. Waiting for me in the colours and I bursting with excitement.

"Anyway you must have thought about it," I said.

"What are you getting at?" His eyes narrowed.

"I'm just saying if you think you'd be afraid, you must have thought."

"Would you get outa that, you stupid lug. Are you reading them books again?"

"I'm reading them books because I'm not going to end up like you," I shouted at him. "I'm going to be somebody. I'm not going to end up in a council house."

His face got red and blotchy. He was going to lose his temper.

"I'm only tryin' to learn things," I said.

"Like what for instance?"

"I'm reading about this man dyin'. How afraid he is and then when he knows for sure he's not afraid anymore."

He leaned both arms on the table and spread his hands flat on the cloth. "When he knows?"

"Yes, you see according to this story it wasn't the dyin'. It was the fear of not knowing that terrified him."

"What do you mean you're not going to end up like me?"

"I'm going to do things. Like I might travel all over the world or become rich."

"Is that so now? And what if I say you're not going anywhere?"

I leaned over until my eyes were level with his. "In another five years I'll be twenty-one and there'll be nothing you can do about it."

"Show me that book," he said.

I went upstairs and brought the book down to him.

"This is what you read then?"

"No. Not all the time. I change around."

"You want to learn things, eh!" he jeered.

"Yes I want to be educated. I might start going to night school."

He flicked through the pages. Then he tore a fist of them out and threw them on the floor.

"What'd you do that for?" I shouted. "What's the harm in me readin'?"

"You're a gobshite, that's why. You'll never get anywhere. You haven't a brain in your head."

I picked up the book and he started laughing.

"You're not funny," I said. "You know that? You're not funny at all."

Willy stands up and goes over to the window to pull the curtains across.

"It's already dark out," he says. "What time is it?"

"It's five o'clock," Joseph says.

"Here sit down and drink your tea," Ma says, passing him the cup.

"God he was stiff as ice," says Willy.

Joseph goes over to the table and pours himself a cup.

"Did you make all the arrangements?" he asks, his voice crisp and harsh from trying to hold back the crying.

"I told you twice already, I've done everything." She shakes her head impatiently the way she does when she has to repeat herself.

"He's coming to get us Mammy," I said.

"Who, Sara, who?" she said, shaking me.

"Me and Maggie under the bed where you're a queen."

My Ma was under the bed where she was a queen and then she went off and left us. So the next time she called me I pretended not to hear.

"I hate everything," I said to Maggie. "I hate the whole world."

Willy gets up and walks around the kitchen.

"I thought if I shook him hard enough he'd come to," he says. "He looked so set on the floor like he'd decided he wasn't goin' to move off it. An' I kept shakin' an' shakin' him an' all the time I was shakin' a dead man."

"It was the way he fell," Ben says. "Must have gone flat down on his face. Over there," he says pointing to where Joseph is sitting.

Joseph gets up off the chair and sits down beside the fire.

"For Christ's sake would you two shut up," he says.

"It's a pure miracle I came home at all," Willy says.

"Ben, answer that knock, will ya?" Joseph says. Ben gets up and opens the back door. Two of the neighbours file past him with their heads bent low.

"Esther," Mrs. Turner says, pulling a chair up beside her. "I was on my way to the shops and Mary comes running down after me. 'Ma, Mr. Kavanagh dropped dead with a heart attack,' she says. And I come immediately." She clutches Ma's hand in her own like she was praying over her.

Ma looks up into her face and then looks away again as if there was something in that face she couldn't bear to see. Mrs. O'Brien nods her head in agreement with Mrs. Turner and sits down.

I make tea and listen to their goster.

Ben answers the second knock on the door and more neighbours file in. I make tea and listen to their goster. 'Oh humey fraw!'

Ma sits quiet like a thought in the back of your mind. She stares out through the window as if she is looking for something. Watching and waiting like she did all those years, as if now that it's happened it doesn't matter because she's still watching and waiting.

"What did you bring that priest into this house for?" she raged.

"I swear to God I never told him anything. I was depressed, that's all. He noticed it in class and said he'd call around to the house sometime."

"You little bitch." Her hand stung my face. "You were trying to make a show of me. God knows what lies you filled him up with."

I couldn't stop crying. She hit me again. And I thought, 'I could lift her quite easily. She's smaller than me. I could mash her into the ground.' But I couldn't because I smelled her. I smelled my mother where she couldn't cry.

And he lies in the hospital morgue on a trolley not giving a tinker's curse for the dark shadows under her eyes or the thin gaunt face staring into the blackness. And not a tinker's curse for me either, that bleeds inside listening to the hypocritical dumdums around me. To drive me insane is what they have come for. No more, no less than to see me ranting like a lunatic as well I may before this wake is over.

His skin was the colour of a pale translucent bulb and his eyes like two carefully drawn chalk lines. A faint tinge of purple showed through the skin on the flaccid mouth, lying flat like a dead fish on a sandy dune. And my eyes eating up every crease and line. Joseph bent over and kissed that mouth. He kissed that dead mouth! I thought my bones would fall out through my skin I shook so much. I thought, 'I'm goin' to drown now, right this minute.' It was the dead fish that did that to me. And Maggie was moaning. Oh! God, I could hear her getting louder and louder. And I turned and ran out into the corridor.

And now on this night. A carousel in a kitchen. Faces familiar. Tongues saying the right words. Bodies move listlessly side to side on the kitchen chairs. They leave one by one. Having said the correct soothing phrases. Relief in the flickering eyelids of my mother. Denies it with a smile. Her tongue says, "Thank you, thank you for coming." Relief, even the kitchen seems to breathe more easily. Always say the right things at the right time. Death is here now. In between the memories. Throbbing! Throbbing! For the only death that really matters, the one that sucks the blood — my own. All else a constant reminder of the ticking clock.

To sing a lullaby, hush now, hush now. It's not the words that flow from mouths. It's not the eyes that smile, or the hands that touch. Touch lightly now, touch tightly now. These people. I have yet to hear one of them scream. Will someone please scrrrrrrrrrream?

Willy leans back on the chair. The front legs rise high. The hind legs swivel and turn, turn and swivel. They keel over like two drunken ballerinas and he sails over the chair and lands on his back. The hum of voices stops and everyone turns to look at Willy lying on the floor. Maggie starts to chuckle and I give a quick cough. He lies on his back looking up at the faces looking down at him. The tears storm down his cheeks. He starts gasping as if he's about to choke on his crying.

"He's dead. My Daddy's dead."

Joseph gives him a hand to get up but he shakes him off and struggles up himself, still crying. He runs through the hallway and up the stairs.

"Poor fella," Mrs. O'Brien says. "He must be terrible upset."

"Go after him an' see he's alright, Sara," Joseph says.

He lies on his old bed, his body stretched the full length, his feet dangling out over the edge. His eyes are all red and puffed.

"I kept thinkin'," he says. "The way he'd laugh when we'd queue up for pocket money on Sundays. And how sometimes he'd meet me after school and bring me for a drive."

When he went to England Ma said, "You drove him out of the house with your fists."

"He shouldn't have done it," Da said. "I won't put up with his carrying on like that."

"And the way we used to all sit around the wireless listenin' to the football results," Willy said.

"He thrashed us all the time when we were small," I say.

His hands thrashing me all over and I thinking this is better than being dead. Better. Better. Better.

"Only when we were bad," says Willy. A half-smile plays around his mouth as if he's gliding over the surface of memories, stopping and moving on over the polished surface, seeing and not feeling because he's moving so fast.

"Sara, do you remember the carnival?" he asks.

"Yes," I say. "I remember it." The carnival shone out through his skin, his dead eyes, his dead nose. And the music played on his purple tinged lips. The music flowing through the loudspeakers bobbing over people's heads like big coloured balls. And his colours spread like a rainbow across the field. Did you know? Did you know he was a man? Your father was a man. Did you know that?

Chapter 2

ESTHER – MARCH 1970

Every tick saying, "You will not sleep. You will not sleep." And me saying, "I will. I will get the better of you yet!" Time, not her. Lies, lies time and her. Close my eyes now and listen to more tick-ticks, nothing, but tick, tick, tick, get the better of you yet. Sleep, sleep, come quick now. Curled up on my side waiting to best you. I hear cars going by. God blast, they're roaring past for twenty-odd years and I never noticed. You become immune. Your ears grow numb, so you think, until one dark night you hear a finger-nail scraping on the wall. Then you know it's going to be one long screech of a night. Wait, I hear that car. That's the same car went by a minute ago. I'd swear it's the same one, driving up to the top of the hill and turning down again. And up again! Y'hear that? It's coming down again. I hear ya, you bastard. You think I don't know you're the same one. Well think again because I know when someone's out to get me. No, not innocent anymore. No, she was not. When they reach their teens they think you're a gombeen. What? Oh! yes. A week I told her, then out of my sight. Out, out, out. But I made a mistake. The following day I told her what I meant was a week from the day of the funeral. That meant Saturday. "Any particular time?" she said. "I know how you like to be precise." I kept my mouth shut. I wasn't going to be drawn out by that bitch. I wasn't going to lower myself any further than I had to. If I didn't know, I'd say she was no daughter of mine. She would tell me nothing. So I was forced to search through her handbag a few times. By chance I looked up into the mirror. I forgot it reflects into the wardrobe. "Satisfied

are you?" she says. "Find what you're looking for?" Her face
all red with temper. Well, we know where that comes from,
don't we. I don't even bother to say because being a mother
means you have to excuse yourself for living and I'm not
about to. Coming home every night and locking herself away
in the bedroom. All day Sunday too. The kitchen wasn't
good enough. Wouldn't even bother to talk except, "Pass the
salt please." "Yes, here it is." That's my daughter wanting
the salt. Haven't heard your voice since yesterday's "Pass the
salt, please!" And then she wonders why I have to go searching through her bag. I heard her laughing two years ago. How
could I forget? Joe was upstairs painting the ceiling and I
heard the two of them talking and laughing, so I went into
the hall to listen and there he was telling her dirty jokes. The
two of them. Oh! yes, it would take filth and dirt to make
her laugh. Pure skin to mine, almost scabby, you might say,
with lines, more precisely wrinkles. You can count my years,
fifty-three, by the wrinkles, fifty-three. What is pure skin
with THAT in her. She can hide where she likes but I can see
THAT. Not the lily if it ever was, I don't believe. I should
have known better with his blood in her.

I don't know meself having the first week over me. The
morning's dragged a bit but by tea-time I wondered where
the day had gone to. I sat most of the time, I kept saying,
"I'll drag myself out of the chair and start tidying up. Any
minute now, I will." But I didn't. That went on all week until
yesterday. Yesterday, I never sat down once and now I can't
sleep at all. I don't often have this trouble. Usually I walk up
the stairs, turn the light on, take my clothes off, get into my
nightdress, turn the light off and goodnight until the following morning. Oh! I didn't polish the floor. Even in the dead
of the night I can smell the place dirty. It's not like me not to
finish a job once I start. Wasted my time trying to drill that
into Sara's head. One time she started knitting a cardigan and
then she threw it aside. I got on to her about it but it's still
lying in the drawer. Typical of her! But I won't upset myself
thinking about her slovenly habits. The floor, I was thinking
about the floor. Alice Turner called in the middle of the
cleaning to see if I was all right. It's as good an excuse as any
to have a look around the house. That one's always putting

her nose in where it doesn't belong. I made her a pot of tea.
That fooled her. Kept her tied to the kitchen table. She
started on about Joe before the cup reached her mouth. What
a good husband he had been and such like. Oh yes, all my
days and nights shut up in the loneliness and I had to learn to
live with it because no one gave a damn and when it was all
over they came and asked me if I was all right. They knew it
was safe then. It was too late. They could sweet-talk their
mouths off and they wouldn't have to do anything but drink
my tea and criticize my house. When they asked me if I was
all right they knew the answer before I said it. But they asked
anyway because it made them feel good. They could go home
then pleased with themselves for doing me a favour when in
truth they'd done nothing at all.

The gas! Did I turn it off? I must have. I filled the bottle
and set the table for the morning and moved the chairs back
from the fire. I must have turned the gas off when the kettle
boiled. Yes. No. If I go down I'll be wide awake. I must have.
I'll count. That'll make me sleep. I'll imagine sheep jumping
over the fence. Some say that does the trick. Six long coffins
leaping over the fence, one died how many was left? The
soul is supposed to go on forever. Up, down, it doesn't
matter. It still goes on. "Let us pray for the soul of Joseph."
"What do you believe in then?" he said. "Nothing," I said.
"When you die, you die." He always got worried about
dying around Christmastime. He ate too much. He thought
he'd never live to see another Christmas so he could stuff
himself again. You can work everything out from Christmas.
Father died eight months after it and Joe — what date is it
today? Yes, two months after it. I always hated Christmas
myself. Extra work. Watching their eyes rolling around in
their heads with excitement and their tongues drooling over
the turkey. Extra work, that's all, work, work, work, so that
their eyes and tongues could slobber in their heads. Think!
They are my children. Isn't it a nice thing to see. And I
slaving over their slobbers. Who will for me? That's what I
asked myself. Who will . . .?

"You must believe in God at least, Esther," Joe said. Sara
was listening at the time and she said, "Why do we have to go
to Mass when you don't?" It was true I didn't believe but

you have to live with people. You have to learn that this is not a free world. You spend all your time doing things you never wanted to do in the first place and no one ever thinks to ask you. All you can do is lie quiet. The reason I wouldn't give in and go to Mass even for appearance's sake was because I had lain quiet so many nights listening to him sweet-talking me, trying to fill up the empty space that couldn't be filled with any man's sugary words. Because a man will say what he thinks you want to hear and he will go on saying it until the words rot in his head, until they become nothing more than the vain heavy breathing that lies under the real meaning of his sugary words. The first Sunday I stopped going to Mass Joe took it as an insult. But he didn't matter at all. My refusal went far beyond his vain heavy breathing. I had found the truth my mother had sprung upon me without ever knowing it. How a woman was dead before she was even born. How she would go on giving birth to the dead, nursing the hatred to her breast, so she would never be allowed to forget. And I gave up God the same way He had given me up.

Where is she at this hour? If he was here she wouldn't. That's the first time I said that. "If he was here." I knew he wasn't but it's the first time I said it and knew at the same time. I didn't think about it. I said he was dead but I didn't say he wasn't here. He could be downstairs because he never came to bed until Sara was in. But he isn't and he isn't in the toilet farting all over the place either. Pa Curran was there, Nancy wasn't. What was that? Yes. He came over to me after the service and said she had the flu. I'm certain he said that she would call to see me this week. And all the others. Hold my breath in waiting! And Mother! "Mother, Joe is dead." "I'm very sorry to hear that, Esther." Not a tear. Not a single one. When Father died she cried. Cried not sniggered. "How do you do? I'm your mother. I believe your husband is dead." As near as possible that would be it. Concern. Oh yes, be concerned and snigger at the same time, as you say it. Just say I hadn't told her. Say I had gone ahead with the funeral and told her afterwards, or, better still, waited and let someone else tell her. "Esther, a stranger had to tell me my own daughter's husband was dead." Martyr praying over the coffin with the rosary beads dripping out of her fingers.

Four years after Father died I went down to see her. She was hiding behind the curtains and I had to call out a few times before she dared open the door. Good enough for her. Frozen stiff in her own terror the way I was. "When I think of all I did for you, Esther," she said. "'I went without myself so you wouldn't go hungry and you left me here all alone." That's right. I left you on your own. That's right.

Peggy Reilly said, "It must be lovely to have a daughter to share things with." Yes lovely! "Where are you going?" "Out." "Who are you going with?" "No one." "What's his name?" "I said I was going with no one, didn't I?" Yes. Lovely, Peggy, lovely. He thrashed her and I could see the brazen look leaving her face with each stroke. The whites of her eyes turning bloodshot as she knotted up tighter on the floor. Now, you will feel it, not know it, feel it. But she was as brazen as ever afterwards. Her selfish little self brazening on until the white would be all gone. God, I keep sickening myself with things that don't matter a damn. I'll start afresh. That's what I'll do. Fifty-three is not too old to start. I'll get my hair done and join an evening class. That's not such a good idea. I'm too old for that. Maybe I'll find a little job. Get me out of the house for a change. I look it, though, I know I look old. What does it matter? It's not as if . . . Peggy Reilly is getting old-looking. How old would she be? Thirty-five, she said, when Peter died. That would make her two years younger. God, no one knows the demands children make on you. Tomorrow I'll sort out his clothes. Imagine opening the wardrobe and seeing his suit. I must contact that man about the insurance. They'll probably try to do me out of some. Try, go on, try it. Pa Curran said the ladder in the shed belongs to him. I don't remember that? It's been lying there two years now. I'm sure Joe would have said. You'd think he'd have a bit of respect and wait. Vultures the lot of them. That insurance man said there were complications. They don't want to pay up. I'll complications him, if he tries to do me out of a penny.

"Daddy put a dead rabbit in my bed," Sara cried. "A dead one Mammy. A dead one." "How could you frighten the child like that?" I said. "It was only a joke." I do. I do. I do. Do you? For how long? For as long as it takes to say "I do."

"I believe in nothing, you hear me? Nothing."

A month before Betty died Joseph was born. I lay awake all night thinking of how I was damned and before he stirred I heard him cry in the wake of her death. "Have you ever been in love?" Betty said. "I'm married, amn't I?" "Yes, but have you ever been in love?" And then I lay in the coffin beside her, "I'm dead now, Betty," I said. "I'm dead. Now you know all about love." I miscarried once. I sat on the toilet and watched the blood roll. Thick and red it matted and clung to the hairs on my legs. I flushed it down and watched it shoot up with the gush of water and then slide down the bowl. One for me. The rest are yours. What time is it? What was I thinking just then? What was it? What's that, the clock? No. What? A creak on the stairs? Is someone there? No, it must be the wind. Word could have got around. You can never tell. Wouldn't put it past any of the black-guards around here. Peggy said that Peter was only a month in his grave when someone broke in. A nice thing to be telling me. I'll count. That's what I'll do. One. Two. Three. Four. Five . . . . Oh! I can't be bothered. Either I can or I can't. What was I thinking before? Yes, the miscarriage. That was a lie. I wanted to, though. I might have and I didn't know. No. I would have known. It's nearly the same thing though, want-ing to. Yes, you could say it was the same thing. But I would have told him. I would have delighted to tell. But maybe I wouldn't. I might have kept it a secret and when he beat me it would have been a judgment on him. Yes, you could say I did. I miscarried. I sat on the toilet and watched the blood roll. I did.

Think about her. Spit. Think about her. Four of them. Each one coming out of an empty night. Sullied nights I called them. When I lay beside him listening to the sugary words and the greasy slick voice, "sullied, sullied," swung back and forth in my head. I tried to think of other words. His name. My name. But I'd grow cold even though I wasn't. Joe, Esther. Joe, Esther. Swing, swing, swing. But they didn't mean anything. They were just two big gaping holes in the darkness filling up the space that couldn't be filled. When he beat me I tried to think of my name on its own. I'd think,

Esther, Esther, so much the words beat in my head the same way he beat me with his fists. And then it wasn't a word at all. It was a pain, an endless screeching pain that wouldn't go away. The children could do nothing about the nights, but at least the days were safe. I could forget in the dirty clothes and stomachs waiting to be filled and the shoes dragging the muck in off the streets, washing the floors for a second time in one day so I could just crawl into bed and not have to think. Daughter, my Sara. Sara, my daughter, daughter, daughter, daughter. The one who came nearest to filling up that space. Looking across at her sleeping soundly and thinking of the lily. Sara, the word meant something. It wasn't a big gaping hole like all the other words. It stretched out in my mind S.A.R.A. Each letter was a word, a meaning in itself, and I thinking sometime I will take it and plant it in Father's garden. A white flower growing out of the green stem. My lily growing week by week, filling my arms, her skin against mine. The nights "sullied, sullied", came back to me, I'd look over at her and feel clean again.

God, I'll never sleep now. I can't remember from one minute to the next what I'm thinking about. Maybe I'm not, maybe I'm just lying here waiting to . . . I won't say that word again. I won't. You can think . . . all night long and never once . . . . No. I won't say and then I might. I could fool it. I could keep saying, "I don't care if you never come." It might fall into the trap then. It won't if it knows you want to. One morning I couldn't stand it any longer. I got up at five and by nine the house was spotless. That did me good and I wasn't a bit tired after it. I'll think. I'll think. I'll concentrate and think things out. I've a lot to think about with Joe gone. I don't say I won't miss him. He changed a lot the last few years. Two heart attacks. That quietened him down. He wasn't so handy with the fists then. I told her to get out. But I said that. I must have said that a hundred times. "I won't have you say those things to me." "We weren't brought up. We were dragged up," she said. Her father not a week in his grave and she said that. "Dragged up!" "We were dragged up not brought up." "Dragged up!" "You don't care," she said. "All you cared about was keeping the house clean and lyin' to the neighbours. The time Willy took the pills you told everyone he had the flu. You even told yourself. You made yourself believe what you told the neighbours. You said it and then you said 'That's right. He didn't take pills at all. He has the flu.' That's what you said. You left him lying in the bed. He could have died and you wouldn't have cared." "Who do you think you are, you slovenly bitch? I'll give you one week to get out of this house. One week, do you hear? Do you hear me, Sara?" "Yes I hear you. I hear you. I hear you." "Do you?" "For how long?" "For as long as it takes to say, I do, I do, I do!" "He's a bastard. That's what." "Who is?" "Sara, am I talking to myself again? I said your effin father's a bastard. He's been talking to you, hasn't he? Well, what did he say about me? Filled you up with lies I suppose. Oh! yes, trying to turn you against me." "No, he wasn't. We went for a drive, that's all." "What was your father doing bringing you for a drive? Don't tell me. The bastard." "He wasn't Ma. I swear he wasn't. He just said he didn't understand you." "Oh! he said that, did he? Jesus that's rich coming from him." "He says you keep filling him up with fries when you know he's supposed to be getting his weight down." "Do you know what he'd do if I dished up a boiled egg, do you? Do I have to tell you what he'd do with that egg?" "I don't want to listen. I don't want to hear anymore. I'm sick listening to you going on about him." "I'm right then, amn't I? After all these years you're on his side." "I'm not on anyone's side. I don't want to hear, that's all."

I can hear Willy snoring. I should have shut the door, I wouldn't have to listen then. If I sleep through the alarm he'll miss the boat. He should never have gone to England in the first place. Trying to cod me, telling me he's earning fifty pounds a week. And not a stitch on his back. I was dying once with the same sickness Betty had. Yes. Five years after her I was here in this bed, the same mattress. If it could talk it'd scream. I was here anyway, thinking I'm thirty-two. It's too young, and then I'd think forty-two, fifty-two, sixty-two and so on until age was no excuse for living because each year would be the same as the one before it. Sara used to come and stand in the doorway. Fidgeting four-year-old swinging her hands behind her back, standing on one foot and changing over to the other when she'd lose her balance. She'd funny eyes. They'd dart around the room. Then fix on one spot, just staring. I'd catch her staring at me, too. Sometimes she'd look as though she was staring right through me. She gave me the willies. Oh! yes. They fill your arms and take away the emptiness for a while but in the end they leave you, and go their own way. With them or without them you end up alone. I remember that year in hospital. I was looking forward to dying. I'd think of them in my arms from time to time filling up the space. But the space went away. It grew so big at one stage I thought I'd fallen right into it. But one day I couldn't feel it anymore. I could hardly remember what it had been like. And then Joe, My God, he gave me a missal. While I was getting ready to die he was out galavanting with other women. A missal, Jesus Christ, a missal to hide his tramps behind. But I didn't die. I never got over that. The day I came home I felt strange. I found the children strangest of all. I'd forgotten I was a mother. I knew I was, but it was only a word we used when we were lying on our backs shut away in the hospital. They sat on the floor, the four of them, staring up at me. And then the bawling started. I wasn't able for it, I was so weak. Joseph turned on Sara and kicked her and she started crying. I picked her up but she got worse. Eventually I had to slap her myself to shut her up.

You never can tell with a man. When I told him Sara hadn't had a period for six months and wouldn't go to the doctor, he did nothing. She could have destroyed our name the selfish bitch. "You better teach her a lesson," I said. "She's gone to skin and bone." "It couldn't be that then," he said. Oh! God I'm onto it now. I can see myself walking up the hill with the shopping bag of messages wearing me out. Willy was leaning over the wall calling to me. "Sara's sick. Sara's sick, Ma, come quick. There's a man in the kitchen brought her home." And then to see that funny look on the man's face. To face that man and say, "Thank you for bringing her home. It must be a bad cold." And he saying, "Not at all. It must be." He must have thought I'd raised a house full of blackguards. Full of lipstick and black eyes and I thinking, 'Is she? Is that why?' I wouldn't have been surprised because you could see THAT in her. But I was spared.

God knows what was wrong. I could have killed her then with her sullen face turned into the pillow refusing to say a word, not caring about all the worry she was causing. My whole life sacrificed for them and they wouldn't do a thing for me. I made her get up and I brought her down to the doctor. I told him straight out she hadn't had them for six months and I thought she might be. I refused to leave the room while he examined her. She'd fool God Almighty if she got the chance. As I say it turned out she wasn't. But she wouldn't say, she just let me drive myself up the walls with worry. "You've got to give her a good thrashing," I said to Joe. "She won't speak to me. You've got to bring her to her senses." "What good would it do to thrash her," he said. He took her side against mine! All the beatings he gave me were nothing compared to those words. I couldn't believe it. Jesus, all the times he thrashed her without giving her a second thought. When he said, "Leave her be," I thought 'What would you know? What would you or any man know.' But I got her in the end. Daughter a namow, namow, daughter, namow. Say it again, namow, namow, namow. One night she didn't come in until four in the morning. "Do you know what's going to happen to her one of these nights?" I said. "I'll kill her if it does," he said. "I'll kill her with my bare hands." That's right. When she came in he was sitting up in bed waiting. He let her have it good and proper because she's got to learn. "Whore," he shouted at her. "You fuckin' little whore," beating it out of her. That's right. That's right. It would take a sledge hammer. For her own good. You whore! Whore! My daughter. Namow, namow, white island. Where is the white island. 'Beat it out of her. Go on. Beat it out forever.' It's not me. It was not me because I scrubbed it away with the nailbrush until it bled. 'Thrash her. Go on! Thrash her, Joe. Beat THAT out of her. You hear me? Beat THAT out of the little whore.' I could feel the hands thrashing me, cleaning me out to get ready to bleed for a long time. Until it's washed away and I can see the white for myself. 'Thrash her, Joe, thrash her. Beat it out of the dirty bitch.'

Oh! that bloody clock. Tick, tick, tick, Joe is dead. I should feel something. I should cry. It would relax me, tire

me out. I can't cry. When Father died I did. That's the last
time I remember doing it. Your father is . . . . Father is . . . .
Is Father dead then? Not Betty. Father. Twelve years later.
Not your mother, or your sister, your Father. Is he? He's
not Kevin Lee. Kevin Lee is Kevin Lee, but my father is my
Father.

"The best of fuckin' luck to him," Joe said. "Your mother
turned him into a weed. He's in the best place now." "You
have to put an F in front of everything and everything is the
same as your words."

But he's gone now. Joe's dead. He's dead in the brown
coffin under the graveyard. Tomorrow Sara goes. But I have
Ben. He's a good boy, the only one with a bit of considera-
tion in him. "There'll be just the two of us soon, Ben," I
told him. "We'll do the house up in a few weeks. Get a bit of
light into the place for a change." He's a good boy my Ben.
He wouldn't leave me, not like the others.

I felt his heart. It was stopped, no sound, no flicker. His
skin, a funny thing, flopped, dropped on the lino when we
came in.

I must have dozed off, I don't remember her coming up. In
the bed where I could look over and see her. My daughter.

The white island, a smooth-faced earth where I had to
clean myself thoroughly before I set foot on it and I thinking
they will know. They will smell it off me. I let the water run
down me. It was freezing but I suffered the cold and waited
for the glow to come. I knew it would come back if I waited
long enough. I didn't even bother to dry myself off. I walked
up the hill to the ridge that swept down into the valley. The
grass was as white as my marble skin. I reached up and
touched the trees as I passed by, invisible to the eye because
white was upon white. When I reached the ridge I started
downwards and the doors of the white cottages began to
open. As I approached the first one, figures in white cowls
filed silently out. As the last one came through the door I
was upon them and I stepped into line behind the last figure.
They began walking. Then they slowed down. They stopped
altogether. The last figure in the column turned around and
faced me. As it did the cowl fell to the ground. It wasn't an
it, it was her. My daughter, Sara, staring through me as if she

didn't recognise me. She turned and walked in the direction I had come from originally. The column of figures started walking again but as I began to follow them the path started to crumble. The white path started sliding down under the ground and the brown earth appeared in its place. The lily, the lily was embedded in the brown murky earth. My white lily growing out of the dirty earth and not out of the white. Up on the hill I could see Sara standing looking back down the valley. I hurried after her and grabbed her. They'd sent her away. She'd never be purified now. So I told her to get out. "I'll get the better of you yet," I said. And I did. I told her to get out.

"Out," I said. "Out, out, out of this house."

Chapter 3

SARA – JULY 1958

We all said that when we'd meet each other out we'd pretend
we never saw each other before. It was my idea. I wanted to
pretend I didn't live where I did but I couldn't do it if everyone knew I had scruffs for brothers. You'd be able to tell
right off I was a nothin' when you'd see them. Sometimes I'd
walk down the town and pretend I wasn't there but I'd see
one of them coming up towards me and they'd go an' spoil
everything.

What I really wanted was to pretend I wasn't real. I'd
know I was, but sometimes I got this queer thing comin'
over me and I'd feel I was in the place. It was the kind of faraway place where you didn't want to cry and you couldn't
see yourself. You'd kind of feel like you could see everybody but they couldn't see you. Maggie was in the faraway
place all the time. She lived on the wall over their bed and
sometimes if they weren't there she'd come down and sit
beside me.

Joseph said that he heard Mammy sayin' I was terrible odd
because I didn't play with the other girls on the hill. She was
always saying things like that about me. But I don't like
playin' very much, I like to just sit somewhere and watch.
Like right now, I'm sittin' on the bench against the wall of
the playground so I can see everybody comin' an' goin' on
the hill. The playground is a square of concrete but nobody
plays in it because it's too small. Across the road Ben an' two
fellas are skittin' around with a ball. One fella dribbles it in-
an'-out between his feet. Ben and the other fella close in on
him, kickin' like mad with their shoes. A man walks past me

an' on up the hill. When he reaches the top he disappears
down the other side. If you close your eyes you can't see.
You're blind then.

I told Mammy about seein' people and then how I couldn't
see once they went over the hill an' that made me want to
cry.

"What's there to cry about?" she said. "You'll see them
again tomorrow, won't you."

"But now I can't see them," I said. "An' my eyes are
watchin'. It's like they never were at all. Not gone away.
They never were."

Ben gets the ball an' circles around the two fellas. Then he
kicks it out past them into the middle of the road an' he goes
runnin' after it.

"Hey Ben," I shout. "Get off the road or I'll tell. You'll
be killed by a car. Ben, I'm warnin' you." He keeps on
runnin'.

"Shut up, Fatso," he shouts across and the two fellas start
laughin'.

"Fatso, Fatso," he shouts again and then he kicks the ball
back to the laughin' fellas.

"You're getting more like your daddy every day," Mammy
said. "A real little puddener. He has to have a car. He's too
fat to walk anywhere."

"I'll break your fuckin' mouth," the Big man said.

"He's your daddy," she said. No. The Big man in the dark.

"You waddle like a duck," Joseph said. The duck was in
the book and the mirror made me a waddle-puddener like
they said.

Willy comes out through our gate an' walks down the hill
with his hands stuffed into his pockets. He can whistle like a
man. His nose sticks out of his face like the peak of a cap on
a man's forehead. When he gets a cold you can see the snots
stuck up it. Even when he blows he leaves a bit behind.

"You leave him alone," I said. "You hear me. He's my son.
My son."

He crosses over to the other side of the road and when he reaches Ben and the two fellas he turns off up into the side road.

"Where you goin' Willy," Ben shouts after him, but he keeps on walkin' and doesn't look back.

"What are you so mad at him for. He's only whistlin'," I said.

"He has me worn out," she said. "I can't bear to see him that way."

"He's mine. You leave him alone. He's only whistlin'." Then I could hear her downstairs. The face in the bars was all pink and soft like a jelly. I put my hand in an' rested his hand on my fingers. I could feel the soft. He was goin' up an' down under the blankets with the whistle.

"You're my son," I whispered. An' his eyes went bluer, like pieces of sky in his head.

Then she was standin' beside me again.

"What are you doing," she said. "Get away from that cot." And she pulled at me. Kild her dead. Kild her stone dead with a stick.

"He's my son," I said. "An' I'm mindin' him." Laughed. She laughed. Kild her. Kild her dead.

"Now don't be silly. Come downstairs and play."

"I won't go nowhere. I'm stayin' right here with my son." And then she went to, only I saw the hand, so I ran into the corner where she couldn't.

"He's mine," I shouted. "I'm not goin' nowhere."

"Don't be silly now, Sara," she said. Silly. Silly. Silly. Was in the mirror where the Big man was. "Close my eyes, Maggie," I said. "Close them an' you look. 'Cause the night is a secret an' the Big Dark was whisperin' over the bones an kept shakin' them. The snake was standin' up an' Maggie's eyes were lights, only black lights, but she could see an' I couldn't.

Ben comes runnin' over to me. His legs run out in front of his body he's comin' so fast.

"I saw you go into the shop. What'd you buy?" he says.

"I got sugar for Mammy."

"Did you get change then?"

"No. I got none so don't come lookin'," I say.

"Course you got change. Give us a penny," he says.

"I told you I got none. N.O.N.E."

He starts walkin' back up the hill with me.

"When I grow up I'm goin' to be a singer," he says. "Listen to this. Old-Mac-Donald-Had-A-Farm-E-I-E-I-O."

He stood in the middle of the kitchen, his brown eyes shinin' like polished shoes an' his feet tappin' the ground.

"Sit down an' have your tea," Mammy said.

"No. Watch me, watch me first," he said. He danced around the kitchen his feet like birds wings flappin' up and down, sideways up an' down.

"Watch me singin' now." His voice was loud an' he was small. The singin' was bigger than the small.

"Once more. Just watch this last bit," he said. He lay flat on his belly an' pushed his back up into a hump an' he made queer noises.

"What am I?" he shouted. "What am I?"

"You're a clown," Mammy said. "Now come an' have your tea."

"I can sing, too," I say.

"Not as good as me, you can't," he says. "When I grow up I'll be famous." Then his eyes sink back behind his lids an' his body sucks in.

My Mammy has a name.

"Give us a penny," he says.

"I told you. I got no . . . ."

"Yes you did. I know by the look on your face, you did. You can say you lost it. It wouldn't be your fault if it got lost."

"Whose fault then?" I say.

His head goes down like he was searchin' the ground for an answer. Then it comes up again. He pulls his shoulders back straight like a soldier's an' kicks a stone ahead of him with the toe of his shoe.

"I'll be a singer or a funny man," he says. "Look." He hunches his shoulders up like a collar around his neck an' pushes his teeth out under his mouth an' spits on the ground.

"Sara. Watch me, now. Watch me. I'm a monster." He prances around in a circle, growlin' like a dog, his fists flayin' into me.

"Stop your messin'," I say. "I'll let the sugar fall." She has a name. Esther. Ma Esther. Daddy calls her Ma but she's not his Ma at all. Esther. She's my mother.

"Say it. Say it," he says.

"Say what?" I say. "Mind the sugar, mind it."

His fists beat into me chest then he circles around me again an' puts them up like a boxer.

"Say it. Go on. Say it or I'll punch you." His fists come shootin' out at me but he misses an' hits the sugar right out of my hand.

"Now look what you've gone an' done. You stupid eejit." His eyes bulge in his head like two taws as he watches the sugar pourin' out of the split seams an' sinkin' into the cracks in the path.

"What'd you go an' do that for?"

"It's your fault," he says. "You wouldn't say it. Not once, you wouldn't."

He starts to run like the hammers up the hill. I could see her face mad at me so she wouldn't love me with the cold in her bones. Soft, was soft then hard, so I didn't know.

It began to rain. It lashed down on my head an' I could see the sugar turnin' wet like hard pebbles of rain an' seepin' faster into the cracks. An' Ben runnin' like crazy past our house an' on up the hill. Like he never was.

What? Say what? I knew, but he said, "Fatso, Fatso." But I would have when he got mad enough except the sunk look in his eyes when he said it an' I thinkin', 'Sometimes you look like an oul man. A midget that never grew up.' You rot in hell for what you just did, Ben Kavanagh. You just rot in hell.

I turned in our gate and went in the back door.

"It took you long enough," she says. "Where is it?"

"It spilt," I say. "I was comin' up the hill an' a man knocked me down."

She jumps up out of the chair an' grabs my ears.

"You little liar," she shouts.

"O, lemme go. Lemme go. It was Ben. It wasn't me. He spilt it on the ground."

"You stupid bitch," she says, pullin' them harder. "You stupid clumsy bitch. Do you think I'm made of money. I send you for one simple little message an' you let it fall. My God! Can't I trust you one time? Have I to do everything myself? Have I?" She lets go my ears. "Get out of my sight," she says. "Before I kill you."

I run up to the bedroom and write in my head. It comes so fast sometimes I can't think what it is. I remember one thing an' not the rest. Like I can be mad for days and not remember what an' then I do 'cause I write in my head.

I wasn't mad anymore, I was cold like an icy wind hangin' around on a day that didn't want a wind. But I was there anyway 'cause I just was. I could feel the cold in her bones 'cause if she did I would know. I wouldn't be writin' it in my head until it makes me want to scream. The rain was runnin' down the window. The scutterin' rain beatin' on the glass like the words in my head. If she just would then it would be all right. I wouldn't be nobody then 'cause I would feel the soft an' she would be an' so would I. I began to cry low, so she wouldn't hear me 'cause I said I wouldn't ever ask her. It didn't need askin'. It was too big an' I couldn't say it anyway, 'cause she would laugh an' say she did an' I'd say, "Do you Ma? Do you really Ma?" An' I'd still feel like an icy cold wind. It wouldn't be to say. It just wouldn't be. I was afraid to cry in the dark an' Maggie said, "You're a softie. You cry in the day." "That's different," I said. "The day an' the night aren't the same." And they weren't 'cause I felt so heavy with the Big Dark on top of the Little Dark.

We don't have any pictures or ornaments in our house. Mammy says things like that are only dust-catchers. But one day Daddy brought a picture home.

"Pa Curran was goin' to throw it out," he said. "I thought you might have some use for it."

It was a picture of Sacred Heart an' it was put over my

bed.

"He said, 'I love you'," I said. His two hands were stretched out so you'd be able to see the holes in his hands with the blood fillin' up the wounds in little lumps. I told Mother Agatha in school that I'd got me own picture an' she said that Christ died on the cross 'specially for me.

He got himself dragged backwards through hell for me!

Last year I made me Communion in a white dress an' a veil out of a shop. Like a little queen, I was. There was a big parade through the streets on account of the Communion an' I was allowed to walk in front an' carry a big banner. I pretended to meself that I was the Blessed Virgin an' I kept makin' the sign of the cross to the people watchin' as we paraded through the streets. Mammy came over an' whispered, "What do you think you're doin' makin' a holy show of us?" but I made the sign of the cross to her an' pretended I couldn't hear her. I got loads of money, too. I kept openin' me new bag an' lookin' in to make sure I wasn't dreamin'. No, I wasn't. All those lovely pennies an' two-shilling pieces. I hid the money in a paper bag in the press so I'd be able to buy presents at Christmas. The Sacred Heart made me rich. I felt so important, the priest puttin' the Host into me mouth an' everyone sayin' it was my special day an' so it was too, all there in me bag. Yes, anyone who'd give me a day like that must be crazy about me.

But what about the Devil? Mother Agatha is forever tellin' us that if we commit a grievous sin the Devil will come an' burn us in the fires. Yes, I believe that. One time I woke up in the dark an' there he was at the foot of the bed. A big snake with a tongue flickin' in an' out of his mouth. Maggie was lookin' down at him an' she started moanin'.

"Oh take the snake off me bed," I whispered to the Sacred Heart. But Maggie laughed at me. So the next mornin' I prayed real quiet to Sacred Heart to send the snake back to Hell, but he never did.

Maggie was standin' up on the wall in the dark. Even when the Big Dark was over the Little Dark she wouldn't cry. "What you doin' standin' up already for?" I said. "Come down an' sit beside me and hold my hand." She came down off the wall and held my hand. She stroked my fingers one by one. "Tell me," she said. "Tell me." "No," I said. "I don't know nothin'." "And what's nothin'," she said. "Nothin' is everything. The fires of Hell comin' out of my ears in screamin' agony." "That's right. That's right," she said. "Now tell me what I told you about words." "No I'm not sayin' no more. Go back on the wall." "Tell me," she said, her hands still strokin' mine but squeezin' hard at the same time. "A million words is the same as throwin' a stone into the sea," I whisper. "The sea bein' already full of words, drowned and sucked into the sand. The whole world is full of words, and people are rotten sick with the words spoutin' out of their mouths like waterfalls. An' words are rotten with their own words, an' the rotten is rotten with the rotting of words. Why do I have to keep sayin' that, Maggie, why?" I said. But she wouldn't tell me.

"Can I stir it?" I say.

"No. You'll slop it all over the floor," Mammy says. She stirs the spoon around the pot with the lid half on. Each time she stirs it touches the lid and the lid twitches like the blink of an eye an' then settles down again.

"Why don't you take the lid off while you're stirrin'?"

"It cooks better if you keep it on," she says.

My Mammy's name is Esther. I didn't know mothers had names. I didn't know.

"How can you stir proper with the lid in the way?" I say.

She stirs the spoon around three more times.

"Did you do any homework last night?"

"I did a little bit. I don't have to have it 'till Monday. Mother Agatha says I'm the best in the class. She says if I bring the paper in to her every day when you're finished with it she'll give me a penny. Can I bring it in Ma? Can I?"

"Yes, I suppose so. You can bring it in every second day. We'll need some for the toilet." She keeps on stirrin'.

"Where's your Daddy gone?"

"He's out front talkin' to some man."

"Who is it, then?"

"I don't know. Just a man."

"Well call him and tell him the dinner's ready."

I go out through the back door an' call. He stands with his back to me leanin' over the wall.

Ben comes in through the gate an' I follow him in.

"What's for dinner Mammy?" he says.

"Stew. And hurry up. It's nearly ruined waitin' on you. Sara. Did you call Daddy? Well, call him again. The dinner's gettin' cold."

I go out an' call an' he says goodbye to the man an' comes in. I sit down beside Joseph. Out of the corner of his mouth he whispers, "Girls are snot rags." The stew runs down his chin like the snots in Willy's nose an' makes me feel sick. I kick him under the table.

"Sara hit me," he shouts. "She kicked me in the leg."

"Sara, did you kick him?" Mammy asks.

"No. I didn't. He's makin' it up."

"She did so," he shouts. "She kicked me under the table."

Daddy puts his knife and fork down. His face has the red temper in it as he stares over at me.

"What the hell's goin' on between you two?"

"He called me a snot rag."

"No, I didn't. I saw her boxin' an orchard."

"My God! Sara were you stealin'? My God haven't I brought you up to know better," Mammy shouts.

"I wasn't. I was out playin'."

"Who were you playin' with? Go on. Say who?" Joseph shouts.

"I was out playin' with Sheila O'Sullivan," I say.

"No you weren't. I saw you by yourself, boxin' an orchard."

"I was not, I was playin'."

"You bloody little bitch," Daddy shouts. "Why can't we ever have a dinner in peace. I'll teach you to have a little more respect when you're at the table." His hand lashes out and hits me across the face.

"Stop it!" Mammy shouts across at him. "Stop this racket at once."

His other hand lashes out an' my chair topples over onto the floor.

"For God's sake shut up screamin' or he'll hit you worse,"

Willy shouts over at me.

Daddy jumps off his chair an' I keep screamin' an' screamin' an' he keeps thrashin' me. Ben suddenly springs up off his chair an' lands on Daddy's back. He holds on with one hand an' thumps him in the shoulder with the other.

"Leave her alone," Joseph shouts. "She didn't rob no orchard."

I slither across the floor, away from him an' I jump up an' run into the hall an' up the stairs. I throw the pillow off the bed an' bang my face hard onto the mattress.

"Quiet now," Maggie whispers. "Quiet now." She sits on the wall, her eyes flashin' hard like the knife in my belly. Then the cryin' comes, but Maggie keeps on starin' down at me her eyes steady and cold like they were just bidin' their time. Outside the rain is cryin' against the window. Then Maggie starts to wail in the dark, not cryin' but wailin' like an oul' woman.

When Mammy was gone I didn't know. "She's still here," I said. "She's not gone." But then everybody was gone an' she was gone so I was alone. But I wouldn't say it. When she sat in the kitchen, coughin' an' wheezin' an' suddenly makin' for the sink to spit out the red blood it was my blood an' my coughin' I was hearin'.

"For my son," I said.

"No. Not your son. Your brother," she said.

But the red blood was mine too, an' she didn't say "No."

Grandma came to look after us an' Mammy took to the bed. She lay down an' the pillows were bigger than her face. Her face was sunken in like a rotten apple. The room was cryin' but you couldn't see the wet because her eyes were cryin' but the wet couldn't come.

"I'm goin' down for the messages," Gran said. "You're not to go near the bedroom while I'm gone."

"No. I won't go near," I said. She gave me a doll to play with 'cause she didn't know about the soft. As soon as I heard the front gate bang shut I went upstairs. She was flat down under the covers an' when she wasn't coughin' an' spittin' into the basin she would curl up on her side like me.

"It's only me, Mammy," I said. Her head lopped down sideways onto her shoulders an' her eyes stared through me the way the doll's eyes did.

"It's me Mammy. Can I come in?" She shook her head an' it lopped back onto her chest. She stared at the wall facing her as if it was a mirror an' I wasn't in it. Then two men came an' lifted her onto a little narrow bed an' carried her downstairs through the front door an' down the steps an' through the gate an' into a white car. The window was cryin' into my face an' I stroked the glass. Then I ran into the kitchen.

"Where's my Mammy gone, Gran?" I said.

Gran put her arms around me but they didn't smell of her.

"Are you goin' to mind me now, Gran?" I said. "Are you?"

"You poor little girl," she said holding me tighter. Not smelling of her.

"I'm not a little girl," I said. "I'm four. I'm a big girl. Are you goin' to mind me Gran? Are you? Are you?"

Then Daddy came in through the door an' took my hand.

"We'll go for a drive," he said. The others were gone an' I didn't want to. But he made me. He drove to a big house an' stopped the car.

"You'll have to stay here for a little while," he said.

"Will you come an' see me?" I said.

"Of course, I'll come. I'll come on Sunday."

"When is Sunday? Tell me when?" But he didn't say. I walked down a hall but I wasn't there an' no one could see me. Just like she was gone an' she wasn't. A big woman came an' said she was goin' to look after me.

"Tell me when it's Sunday," I said to the big woman. When Sunday came I waited for him in the Visitor's Room. I sat on the wooden bench facin' the door so I'd see him when he opened it. Sometimes my eyes would stray up towards the window an' I'd jerk them back to the green door again.

"Open door," I said. "Open an' make him come. Come. Come. Come." And it was a long time but he never came. The cryin' came up my belly an' into my eyes but still my face wouldn't.

"I'm not here," I said. "I'm not here." And then I wasn't.

One day the door opened an' it was Grandad with the beard. He put his arms around me an' lifted me up an' then my face started to cry. He took me home to his house an' Gran put her arms around me.

Grandad's house had a big garden in front an' an orchard in the back. I sat under the apple trees an' I could hear her in the quiet. The quiet was purrin' in the air, dippin' an' divin' in the folds of the wind. I could feel my fingers touchin' the quiet where it was soft. Then I put my hands up to my face and ran my fingers over my eyes and opened my two fingers so I could see her. But I never told anyone that she had come to live in the orchard.

Ben kicks the ball back to Willy an' he dribbles it between his feet before kickin' it half-way down the school yard.

"Come on. Come on," Joseph shouts. "Just you try to get it past me."

"Kick it straight in, Willy. Go on. Kick it," Ben shouts. Joseph keeps his eyes glued to the ball. He leans over in a half-squat, his hands on his knees, and his head moving from side to side as he watches. Willy kicks it and Joseph runs in the direction that Willy kicked. Then Willy suddenly takes into a run down the yard after the ball but Joseph sees him and catches the ball as he dives.

He thrashed Joseph, I could see he was hurt because he was eleven an' wore long trousers. He didn't thrash Willy so much because of his asthma. Ben an' me cried.

"I told you, Willy," Ben shouts. "You keep tryin' the same oul' thing over an' over. Kick it straight in, you hear me. Straight in."

"Shut your mouth you," Willy says and he wipes his mouth with his sleeve as he runs back into the middle of the yard.

"Give us a try, Joseph," Ben shouts down. "I can do it."

"It's best they go for a trade," she said. "You're nothin' without a good trade to fall back on. That's why schoolin' is so important."

"You? Oh! You'll get married. There's no need for you to worry."

"You're only a girl," Joseph said.

And they laughed, and she laughed too. My Mammy laughed at me.

"Shove off, Ben. You're too small," Willy says. He leans over, his legs apart and his face set as he watches the ball.

"Kick it back to me, Joseph," he says. Joseph kicks the ball into the middle of the yard.

"One more try," he says. "Only one more."

Willy takes the ball up and then he sets it down carefully a few feet ahead of him. He jogs up and down. Then he stops and stares down at it.

"Come on," Joseph shouts. "For God's sake kick it."

"Yes! Kick it. Kick it," Ben shouts. He runs down the yard and leans against the wall facing Willy.

Willy runs backwards, away from the ball. Then he takes a run at it and kicks it hard down the yard. Joseph comes runnin' up to meet it, his arms open wide. It bounces onto his jumper an' he staggers back but he holds it tight.

"Up the goalie," he shouts, jumpin' up an' down. "I won. I won."

"My turn now," Ben says.

"Oh scutter off. You're only a squirt," Joseph says.

"No. I'm not. What about Willy? He can't even breathe."

Willy sits down on the stoney ground and puts his head between his legs.

"Are you all right, Willy?" Joseph says, sitting down beside him. Willy breathes in harsh an' deep an' lets the wheeze out.

"I'll be all right in a minute," he says.

"See. He can't even breathe," Ben says.

"Shut up. He'll be breathin' in a minute," says Joseph.

I could hear him comin' up the stairs. "If you're comin' in, knock first," I shout out. He walks in.

"I told you before about knockin'. How many times do I have to tell you," I say.

"Why should I have to knock," Joseph says.

"You keep sayin' that every time I say you're to knock. It's only right you should. It's my room."

He jumps up on my bed an' bounces up an' down. "No it's not. It's Ma an' Da's room. It's not your room at all. Even if it was I still wouldn't."

"What are you kneelin' like that for?" Joseph says.

"I'm prayin'. I'm a saint an' I'm prayin' to God." I show him the rosary beads around my neck an' I pull my dress up to show him the cord around my waist.

"What's that for?" he asks.

"It's to make up for sinners . . . Mother Agatha says if you want to be a saint you must suffer for others."

"How can a girl be a saint? 'Sides saints have to be dead before they're saints."

"I am dead," I say. I join my hands together like the statue of Our Lady in school an' I close my eyes.

"Now, I'm dead. I can't see you. I am not of this world but of the next."

"You're a funny one," he says, rolling over on his back. "Ma is right about you. She says you're queer."

"She never said that."

"Yes, she did. I heard her say it to Daddy." He pulls the lower lids of his eyes down with two fingers an' blows out his cheeks.

" 'Mad,' she said. That's what." Then he sucks his cheeks in an' starts gurglin'. "Mad! Mad! Mad!"

"You stop that," I shout. "Just you stop. She never said any such thing."

"Yes she did. 'She's on your side of the family,' she said, 'An' all your side are loonies'."

Mad was in the dark. I could hear the screamin' but there was only quiet but still I could hear it.

"Did she really say that, Joseph? Did she?"

He rolls off the bed onto the floor an' puts his hands on his hips the way she does. "What does that girl be doin' up there all day long? I can hear her talkin' away to herself. What is she up to? That's what I'd like to know," he says. He leans over the wooden railing at the bottom of the bed. "Looney! Looney! You're a looney," he sings and runs out the door.

She didn't go to Mass and the nuns said that every family should kneel down after tea an' say the rosary. "God loves me," I said. And she said, "What nonsense! I don't believe any of that rubbish. The nuns are fine ones to talk."

Maggie didn't believe either. But He loves me. He does. He does. I saw the star in the sky shooting down. You could look but you couldn't touch, so someone must have put it there. Someone must have pushed the star out of the sky.

"I'm comin' up," I say. "You'll have to help me when I get up on the wall."

"There's no room," Willy says. "It won't fit the four of us."

"Yes it will. If you're up there so can I be."

"You better let her," Joseph says. "Or she'll tell. Ma will have a fit if she finds out we were on the shed roof."

"All right," Willy says. "Get up on the wall first an' I'll pull you up."

I climb the wall and hold onto the shed at the same time so I won't fall.

"Let your hand off the wall an' pull yourself up," Willy says.

I dig my feet into the grooves then I let my hand free and I throw my leg over the wall so I'm sittin' astride it.

"Now stand up," Willy says. "An' I'll pull you onto the roof."

"It's too narrow," I say. "If I stand I'll fall."

"No you won't. We stood on it. How else are you goin' to get up?"

I stand up straight on the wall and Willy grabs my arm.

"Now put your two hands on the edge of the roof and then you can swing up," he says.

I grab the edge and pull myself up. Willy pulls and I roll up and over onto the roof.

"Watch where you're puttin' your feet. They're stuck halfway down me gob," says Joseph.

I lie down beside Willy. The sun blinds me.

"What are we lyin' here for?" I say.

"To get suntan," Joseph says. "What else would we be doin' on the roof?"

"I don't like lyin' in the sun. It makes me sick."

"Well what you come up here for then?"

" 'Cause you were all here."

"Hey Sara! Willy can't write," Ben says. "I saw him doin' his exercise an' he can't write proper."

"Don't you start," Joseph says.

"I can so," Willy says.

"No you can't. I saw your writin'. It's like a baby's."

I could hear her moanin' an' groanin' so I crawled up the stairs one by one. The lino was slippy an' shiny an' I knew if I fell I'd fall right down the shiny steps but I kept on goin'. When I got to the top I nearly fell but I held onto the door frame round the corner an' pulled myself up so I was standin' straight. She was lyin' on the bed an' she was so big under the pink apron tossin' and turnin' like she wanted to toilet. She saw me watchin' an' her eyes grew big. The white parts bulgin' as if they were about to fall out of her head, but I didn't know if she really saw me or if she wanted to toilet an' couldn't because I knew how sometimes she'd put me on the pot and I'd try an' try just like her an' couldn't. Then I heard someone on the stairs and suddenly a big lady beside me picked me up an' carried me down to the kitchen. She sat me on the floor but I could still hear her moanin' an' groanin' so I lay down like she was an' started groanin' an' pushin' real hard to see if I could make it come for her, but I couldn't. And then I heard her stop and the big lady's voice so she must have or else it went back up. Then I went to sleep and I didn't see her but when I did she wasn't big under the apron anymore so she must have.

Ma got up from the table and went over to the sink. She filled the kettle and put it on the lighting gas. Dad did a fart. A fart is dirty. So is pickin' your nose an' eatin' it. So is pickin' your nose an' wipin' it on your sleeve, but not as bad as eatin' it. Willy eats it. Dad did another fart and Ma turned around.

"Do we have to listen to that? How are we supposed to eat with that kind of carry on?" she said.

"Shut your mouth, woman," he farted again to let her know he was the boss in the house. Her top lip curled up tight and her gums stuck out like liver on a white plate. "Men are arrogant and dirty creatures," she said. "They'll try to fool you. You better learn that. You're never too young to know about men. You marry a rich man and you'll be all right."

She took the kettle off the gas and poured it into the basin in the sink.

"I try," she said. "God knows I try to keep the peace in this house but that kind of carry on makes me sick."

"It takes little to make you sick, now," he said. "Just keep your fuckin' mouth shut."

"I'm not able for this. You know well I'm not."

"What are you on about?" he said. "Are you lookin' for a fight? By Christ, if that's what you want you'll get it." He picked a knife up off the table. "Another word," he said, pointing it straight at her. "And I'll kill you."

"You haven't got the guts," she screamed at him. "Your answer to everything is your fists. A coward's way."

He threw the knife, half-lifting out of the chair as he threw. It whizzed over the table and landed on the ground beside her feet. Her top lip shot down and clenched tight onto the lower one. And the bones in her face sprung up behind her chin. The skin dropped loosely like a crumpled plaster on a finger but the bones stood out on their own thick and strong, shaping her face like the jutting outlines of a ship far out to sea. She bent down and picked up the knife and she came back over to the table. Her mouth was moving up and down as if she was cold. He opened the drawer and took out another knife and cut his fried egg and rasher up in little pieces and began eating. The knife was lyin' in the middle of the table. I couldn't take my eyes off it. She sat down, the skin was back on her bones but her face was small. My son was small.

"Why does he keep cryin'," I said.

"He can't breathe properly," she said, picking him up out of the cot. I could hear the whistle coming from his mouth. Her face was soft and she held him up to the soft and then I was cold.

"Where'd that baby come from?"

"He came from God," she said, laying him back down in the cot.

"Who is he then?"

"My son," she said. "He's my son."

"Where'd he come from?"

"I told you he came from God."

But I could tell by the way she was talkin' that she was lyin'. Big people were always tellin' me lies. Slippin' an' slidin' over words and then smilin' at you so you'd believe. He was my son! My son!

He was sitting in his shorts and she was washin' the clothes, with her lips tight together.

"You are disgusting looking," she said. "Is it too much to ask you to dress yourself?"

She took her apron off and flung it on the floor and ran upstairs. The sun was shining on his skin an' I sat and watched it shining an' then I sat on his mouth.

"I came to tell you," I said to the waves. "He ran away this mornin' and he took me money." The sea was mad for me. She came rushin' up on the sand so I kept tellin' her and she kept rushin' up to me.

"He ran away this morning and they can't find him anywhere," I said. Daddy said, "When I get my hands on that little fart I'll kill him." And Mammy wrung her hands together like she was trying to squeeze the blood out of them.

"He took my communion money with him. God made me rich an' he went and stole it," I said to the sea.

I got a stick and walked alongside the blue railing, hitting it as I went along. Belting that shite good and proper. On the way home I saw Willy lookin' in a shop window.

"You're supposed to be lookin' for him," I said.

"I'll look after it," he said. "I'll clean the white part every mornin' and when I run it on the ground I won't bash it against a wall."

"What are you talkin' about?"

"That lorry," he said. "Ma says I might get it for Christmas."

"He stole my communion money," I said. "He went and stole my good Holy Communion money." I'll tell Maggie tonight. She'll give him the works. The sea knows. I told the sea.

We walked up the town. Willy walked a little ahead of me because his legs were longer than mine.

"I know where he's hidin'," Willy called out.

"Where?" I asked. "Why didn't you tell Daddy if you know."

"He's goin' to kill him," Willy said. He put his hands in his pockets and started whistlin'. We turned up outa the town and onto the back roads. Trees sprouted over the high walls on one side. On the other side the fields stretched out to the mountains. At the end of the straight stretch of road we turned up into a narrow laneway. The wind and the sea and the trees. "Who am I, then?" I asked and Maggie laughed.

Willy picked the leaves off the hedges and stuffed them in his pockets. "Where are we goin' now?" I asked. He broke into a run his long legs boundin' ahead of me and he disappeared around the corner. Over the top of the hill, they never were.

When I turned the corner I saw a small cottage set in behind an overgrown hedge. A red chipped gate led up to it. The roof was bare and you could see the wooden laths lying crossways on it. The white-washed stones of the cottage were blackened by fire. I could feel a light wind goin' up and down me back.

When the fire siren goes the Devil comes into the room.

"I'm a good girl," I said. "The Devil won't come for me. Will he?"

"Well, I'll have to close the door anyway, or he'll get in," Daddy said.

"In here," Willy shouted. "He's in here." Inside the cottage there were rotten pieces of wood lyin' on the floor. For a minute I couldn't see anything it was so black and then the light came an' I could see Ben sitting in the corner beside a fire grate. His knees were hunched up and his arms were tight about them.

"You stole my communion money," I said. "Where is it?"

"Shut up," Willy said. "He's goin' to be kild when Daddy gets him."

A brown bag was sittin' in the fire grate. I picked it up and turned it upside down. Six packets of sweets, two bags of crisps and three apples.

"My communion money! You little fucker! Look what he spent my money on."

"Why'd you run away?" Willy said. "You knew he'd kill you."

"I'm goin' to be famous," Ben whispered. "I'm goin' to be." And he banged his fists up and down on his knees.

"I hope he beats the shit outa ya," I said.

"Come on," Willy said, pulling himself up off the ground. "We better go home."

On the way home Ben kept actin' like he was sick in the head.

"I'll show you all," he said. "I'm goin' to be famous and no one's goin' to stop me."

When we reached the gate he slouched behind Willy and me.

"Will he kill me?" he whispered.

"Yes," Willy said. "He said he was goin' to."

Dad thrashed him and thrashed him. He beat him the same way he beat any of us, but Ben never said a single word. His head kept lollin' from side to side but his eyes were sort-of blank and staring as if he was watchin' himself from the far side of the kitchen and didn't give a God damn. When it was over he walked to the door.

"You can do what you like," he said, "But you'll never

make me cry." And he banged the door shut after him.

There was a silence then. A kind of hush all over the kitchen with his words. Then we heard him jumpin' up and down on the bedroom floor and him shouting, "You'll never make me cry, you hear me. You'll never make me."

Daddy got off the chair and made for the door. "I'll teach that bastard a lesson he'll never forget," he said. But Mammy got in front of him and leaned against the door.

"Leave him alone," she said. "He's had enough for one day."

Later I went up to the bedroom. He lay on top of the bed, his eyes starin' at the light bulb. He lay there like a person that sees and hears nothin'.

"Are you all right?" I asked. But he lay there not minding me with his eyes on the light, not even blinking, like he was staring at nothing. His face was hard and set like a man's. That made me very cold and I got the shivers and I started cryin' inside for him.

I wrote in my head after seein' Ben's face that day. How he would stand in the middle of the kitchen and sing but his hands lay down by his sides and never moved. Then he would sit down as if he'd never stood up at all. Ben is my brother and his light's gone. It went away and he didn't cry because he wasn't Ben anymore. Daddy beat him again and the dead was in his eyes. He sucked in and you could see the dead in his body. He got the messages for Mammy and he didn't let them fall. "He's a great boy," she said. "I'd be lost without him." He followed her around everywhere and didn't go out to play. So then he was worse, he was a shadow in the dead. Ben is my brother, I wrote, an' his light's gone.

I ran on the sand in the dark. The sand was wet and lumpy under my feet but I kept runnin' because I could hear the footsteps behind me. I kept thinkin' he's right behind me. he'll catch up. So I looked over my shoulder. I could see the feet and the shoes but he had no body and no face. No matter how fast I ran the distance between us never got any bigger. Then suddenly it was day-time again an' I was sittin' on the beach buildin' a sandcastle. When I finished buildin' I jumped all over it and kild it. And then it was night again. I was so tired runnin' every time I reached the end of the

beach it grew bigger and bigger so I couldn't get out of the
wet sand. Then my legs fell down and I had to crawl on my
hands and knees and the cryin' was comin' so fast down my
face and it fell into my hands. It was burnin' me and when I
looked down I saw it was red scaldin' blood comin' from my
eyes an' not tears at all. "Don't touch me," I screamed
back at the feet but the feet kept comin' and I was screamin'
so hard I woke up. "It's all right," I said. "It's all right. It's
not the night-time anymore."

"What are we goin' to do?" Mammy said. "He's been sick all
winter. Look at the schoolin' he's missin'. He's never been
this bad before. By the time he's finished in school he won't
be able to read or write."

"What did he say?" Daddy said.

"Nothin' much! The doctors know no more than we do.
'Get him a foam pillow,' he said. 'He might be allergic to
feathers.' Last time he said to keep him away from pollen.
Pollen, how are ya, and not a single flower on the whole
road. And the time before that . . . ."

"Get the pillow, anyway," Daddy said. "There's no harm
in tryin' it."

"You mark my words it won't work. If you ask me it's
his nerves has him the way he is. Where are you two goin'?"
she asked.

"Up to see him for a minute," I said.

"Well don't stay long. He hasn't had a wink of sleep all
night."

Ben an' me climbed the stairs real quiet as if the sickness
began at the bottom step and travelled up.

"Is he goin' to die?" Ben whispered.

"Don't be silly. He's got the asthma. That's all."

He lay on his side, the blankets movin' up and down on
him. The skin on his face looked dragged tight from the
calf's lick of his hair, knobbly and white over the bones. His
mouth was wide open as he wheezed for air.

"Are you all right?" Ben said, sitting on the edge of the
bed.

He started to talk but the wheeze came like somethin'

trapped in his throat fillin' the room like a barrel full of spit.

"Ma says you're to keep the hot-water bottle up to your chest," I said.

"Sara and me are goin' for a walk," Ben said.

He nodded his head and turned around to face the wall.

"We'll see you later," I said.

"Later alligator," Ben said.

We walked down the hill and turned into the back roads.

"It's funny how he can't breathe. Isn't it?" Ben said. "Ma bought him grapes. Did you know that? They were on the chair in that bag."

"Yes I saw them," I said.

"I wish I was sick and got grapes."

"No you wouldn't. It's a terrible thing to be sick," I said.

"Yes I would. I'd get grapes an' comics. I'd give anything to be sick. There's a fella in our class an' he calls his Mammy, Mummy," he said.

"Is he a posh fella then?"

"I don't know. His mother collects him after school every day. All the fellas laugh at him. We'll go in the woods and collect conkers."

We turned into the road that leads to the woods. Ben picked leaves and sucked them and threw them back into the bushes. On the second bend in the road a small stone wall looked down on a stream dividin' two fields.

"Let's sit on the wall," I said. From as far back across the fields as I could see the stream ran. Soft and cool soundin' it gurgled over the branches and bushes in it.

"Lean over and sing a song into the stream," I said.

"No!" He picked a stone off the ground and fired it into the water.

"Aw! go on. Just one verse."

"I said 'No', didn't I? Come on. Let's go to the woods."

"I'm not budgin' one inch 'till you sing," I said.

"See if I care," he said. And he walked on swingin' himself real casual and scuffin' his shoes into the ground. The Big Dark was breathin' and the Little Dark was pushin' its head away.

Ben came back around the bend. "Are you comin' or aren't you?" he said.

I took into a run and he started laughin' and ran too.
"Bet I get there before you," he shouted.

"Get out and look at the well. Make a wish, Sara. No, you boys stay in the car," he said.
I could see their faces in the back window not knowin' whether to laugh or cry when he started the car up without me.
"Run, Sara, run," he shouted out the window. Willy's eyes were crying.
He slowed the car down and when I reached it he started up again. "Run, Sara. Run," he shouted and drove off.
Eight times. "Run, Sara. Run."
"Run, Sara. Run."
He stopped the car but I wouldn't run up to it. So he got out and called "What's keepin' you?"
"It's Christmas, Daddy," I shouted. "You shouldn't do that on Christmas. He hit me across the face and I could hear them laughing in the car. "It's Christmas, Daddy. Not on Christmas."
"Get in and shut up," he said. And I said. "O! Daddy, Daddy!" to the colours. "Oh! love me Daddy, Daddy" to the colours.

"Are you spyin' on me?" he asked.
"I can come around the back of this shed when I feel like," I said. "What's in that tin?"
"A bubble blower," he said. He dipped the wire hoop in again and blew hard.
"There's all colours in the bubbles. Give me a try," I said.
"It's nearly empty now. You seen it. Now go away."
"Where'd you get it?"
"I bought it."
"With what then? You spent all your money on Sunday."
"I did not. I had threepence left an' I bought it with that."
"You're a stinkin' liar, Ben Kavanagh. You went an' stole it. You stole my communion money, too," I said.
"I never did. I'm not a stealer," he said.

"Yes! you are."

"Prove it! Go on, prove it then. See, you can't prove it because I never stole nothin'."

"I'm goin' to tell Mammy you stole that bubble blower," I said.

"I didn't. If you tell Mammy, I'll kill you."

"How'll you kill me? You're only a squirt. I'd knock you flat any time I wanted."

"Don't tell Mammy. Please don't, Sara. I never did anything."

"Well, what you hidin' behind the shed for then?"

"I'm not hidin'. I'm just sittin' that's all, just sittin'!"

"Well, I'll tell anyway. If you didn't it won't matter will it?"

He leaned back against the wall his face all frightened lookin'.

"You're Ma's pet," I said. "You follow her around. Willy says you buy her sweets. If she knew where them sweets came from you wouldn't be her pet no more," I said.

"Yes, I would. She says I'm the best of a bad lot. We're all tainted, she says. What's tainted, Sara?"

"Did she say I was tainted too?"

"She says we're all tainted. You won't tell on me, Sara? Say you won't."

"I'll see. You stole my money. Why'd you steal on me? What'd I ever do on ya?"

"I don't know," he said. "I don't know why I do it." He clenched his fists up in a ball and rubbed his mouth. Then he started to cry.

"Shut up cryin'," I said. "I won't tell, only shut up that cryin'"

I came in through the back door and put my school bag on the chair. The kitchen was empty but I could hear, like the dark in the bedroom, only it was in the kitchen. The Big Dark was on top of the Little Dark. I jumped out of bed an' over to the Big Dark and shook it. Then I wanted to close my eyes so it would be all right. But I couldn't because the Big Dark was comin' for me and the snake was comin' for me so I walked backwards into the black, an' I screamed for the Little Dark but it lay on the bed sayin' nothin'. Then the black was hoppin' up and down in front of my eyes and I couldn't see the snake anymore. "You'll never make me dead," I shouted at the Big Dark. But I was dead. I was fallin' into the dead and the Dark was far away. I opened the door and crept out into the hall and stood on the bottom step of the stairs. Mammy was cryin' loud cries. I moved up tight against the wall so I could see. The two of them were on the landin'. She was kneelin' on the floor and he was bent over her, his two hands around her throat.

"I'm goin' to kill you this time," he shouted. "I've had enough."

"Go on. Kill me. Kill me." She screamed. "I don't care. Kill me, you bastard." She's my Mama. My Mama.

"You bitch of a woman," he said and squeezed real tight on her throat. I wanted to run. He was goin' to kill her, like in the Dark but my mouth was screamin' an screamin' no screams an' I couldn't move.

"Let my Mammy go. Let her go," I shouted up, but still I couldn't move from the wall. He turned and looked down at me.

"Now look what you've done," he said. "I hope you're satisfied."

He threw her on the floor and came runnin' down past me and out through the front door. I ran up to her and helped her into the bedroom.

"He's a terrible bastard," she screamed. "Bastard. Bastard. Bastard."

"You lie down and close your eyes an' it'll be all right," I said.

So she lay down and her face went all white and her mouth curled up. She dug her fingers into my arm.

"All men are bastards," she said. "Say it after me. Say 'All men are bastards.' Say it! Say it, Sara."

So I said it over and over again until her eyes closed. The words goin' round in my head like a clock. And then Maggie started sayin' it for me and she just wouldn't stop. She just wouldn't stop sayin' it.

He bites into his apple an' it crunches and the juice runs down his mouth and onto his chin. He is soft and red an' so is the apple. He winds the car window down and throws the butsy away. He looks out of the window at the fields and the sun. He isn't mindin' me at all. No one minds me 'cause they can't see me. Except his colours, they always mind me.

"Daddy, can I go to the carnival every day?" I say. He turns and looks down at me an' the colours smile.

"We'll see," he says. "You'll have to ask your mother about it."

"When will it come?"

"Next week it'll be here," he says.

"What's in a carnival, Daddy?"

"Oh. All kinds of things," he says. "You'll know soon enough."

The juice is still on his chin and the sun sparkles on it.

"There's spit hangin' outa your chin," I say. He takes a hankey out of his pocket and wipes it away. Then he blows his nose.

"Do you love my Mammy?"

"What makes you ask that?" he says.

"O, I dunno. I was just askin'. Do you Daddy? Do you love her?"

He starts laughin' at me and turns the engine on.

"Jasus, you're a gas character. You ask the queerest things," he says.

I wrote in my head because he brought me for a drive an' I wasn't no one then. He was mine in the car. I could feel the soft except when he laughed at me. "You're to mind me in the soft," I said. The colours were in the car because she wasn't there an' I was. The Big man is my Daddy. My Daddy.

My dress clings to me like a sticky sweet with the heat. Through the kitchen window I can see the blue sky and the sun. I can hear the clock tickin' on the mantel-piece.

"Is it time to go yet Mammy?" I ask.

"Stop gettin' so impatient. We're in plenty of time," she says, rubbing her face all over with the damp cloth.

"Does Daddy own it Mammy?"

"No, he doesn't. Your Daddy helps Mr. Conway to run it. So don't you go botherin' him for free rides."

She puts the cloth back beside the soap dish on the sink and goes upstairs. I can hear her movin' about the bedroom and opening the wardrobe door.

If only she'd hurry.

We walk down into the town. She walks real slow, stoppin' to talk to oul ones and lookin' in shop windows.

"Hurry up Mammy. We'll miss it," I say.

"Take your time. We've got all day," she says. When we reach the end of the town we turn off into Sheaver's road.

"Can I run on Mammy? I'll be real careful."

"Well, all right then, but watch out when you're crossing the road."

I run with the thumpin' in me chest.

The gates of the field are thrown wide open an' I can hear the music. I run like the hammers through it.

"Oh Jasus, just look at them big tents and them flags all round the field, flyin' all over the place. Them people is goin' to fall out. Oh! Look at the chair-o-planes. The music's drivin' me mad."

"Over here, Sara. Look at me."

I look and see Willy sittin' in the swings, yellow ones with red stripes on the sides. He pulls the rope with one hand and waves at me with the other.

Then I am up in the air too, swinging through the air into the clouds. I'm the first in the world to sit on a cloud. Then I go round on the chair-o-planes. Then I try the hoop-la and lose the rest of me money. They fixed it. The field is full of screechin' an' laughin' and the music blares from the loud-speakers fixed to the flagpoles. Waves of heat like colourless butterflies float up and down in front of me eyes. And the bellied half-moons of the swings climb higher and higher in the air. As true as Jasus I'm about to burst. Daddy and Mammy are standin' over by the ice-cream kiosk. His face is laughin' over at me. His eyes are like two fountains with the colours runnin' down his face. All the colours swing in circles around me. Do ya? Do ya?

I wrote in my head real careful 'cause I was so excited. The carnival must be God come down to see us, I wrote. My

Daddy must be something to do with God 'cause all his colours are in the carnival. Everybody laughs. I never saw my brothers laugh the way they do in the carnival. Our house has a smile in it now. Sometimes I tell Daddy a joke. His mouth runs over to me. His eyes laugh lovely at me. His laughin' is like the sun on his tongue. It runs like thick cream across the table to me. Even my Mammy laughs now. She's not a dead shadow anymore, I wrote, she's a little shadow under the sun instead. I'm goin' to laugh forever and forever and so is my Daddy.

"No noise tonight," Mammy says, "I've a splittin' headache. If I hear a sound I'll come up and wallop the lot of you."

"Can we leave the light on?" Joseph asks.

"No you can't. Now up to bed with you."

"That's not fair," Joseph says. "You always let us have half-an-hour with the light on."

"Can we go go to the carnival tomorrow then?" Willy says.

"We'll see. Get up them stairs and lights out immediately. Do you hear?"

In the bedroom there is a quiet. The street lamp shines in like the sun. It comes in long narrow streams through the window as if there was no window, comin' as quiet as the quiet, the long narrow streams throwin' off their own streams on the walls like big starin' eyes. The Big Dark comes into the room. It leans up against the wall, looking at me.

"What you lookin' at me like that for?" I say, but it keeps on comin' over to me. The Dark was always in the other bed and now it isn't. It's comin' for me. I want to scream. My mouth is wide open but nothin' comes out because the Dark is over me with the snake. An' all the colours come down on top of me but they aren't mindin' me. They are eatin' me up. The colours are eatin' me up. And then I'm not me anymore. I'm Maggie. The colours are eatin' Maggie up. So it is all right. It is all right.

Chapter 4

ESTHER – JULY 1958

If I could only have found a place to be quiet in. Some place they didn't know, otherwise I would be half listening for the sound of their footsteps or hear their voices and know they would call out because they would want to know. They would just want to know. Sometimes I raged so much I thought of leaving a note on the kitchen table saying, "Your mother has gone to the toilet. I hope it's not too inconvenient." But then I'd think to myself it's a waste of time and effort. They'll still come looking and I'll hear their damn voices and know there is no place I could go to sit quiet and think.

When he'd come home in the evenings I'd know just by looking at him what was to come. Sometimes I'd purposely pick a fight in the hope he'd leave me alone later. It got so that I didn't have to try. I'd look at him and know, and that sick feeling would start up and I wouldn't be able to stop myself anyway. I knew it was doing no good, that I was just spiting myself because he'd end up beating me and I'd still have to face what was to come later. But I couldn't stop. After he'd go to sleep I'd lie awake thinking how strange it was to hear people passing by the house when I'd just died and no one would ever know because I'd get up when the alarm went off and start another day and it would happen again and again and still no one would know and if they did they wouldn't care and if they did I wouldn't.

Once I stood on the landing half the night rather than lie beside him. I watched the sky turning black the way it does before the heavens open. I listened to the dull shapeless sounds coming out of the night and the sky getting ready to swamp them down under a torrent of rain. As I stood there I thought, quite suddenly too because I was beginning to feel cold and I was going back to bed, 'What is is,' I thought, 'and there's nothing I or anyone else can do to change that.' The time I liked best was when it would become so quiet I'd feel at peace for the first time all day, and I'd listen to my own breathing, calm and unhurried, soothing me with its sounds like the velvet purrings of a cat. I'd imagine the whole world was dead then with the dark rising and quivering before my eyes and think how when he'd be trying to reach me he'd say to me with a kind of puzzled look on his face, "Esther, sometimes I don't know what I'm doing." I wouldn't answer because I knew it suited him to say such things then and that even as he was saying it he was already thinking to blame me. I could have told him he was just wasting his time but he wouldn't understand. He didn't know that he was no more than a black spot in an empty night. I didn't even bother to ask him where he went all those nights. He'd spend an hour in the toilet and come down in his good suit reeking of after-shave and say he was going out with the lads. Or not say where he was going in the good suit, white shirt and tie and tell me to polish his shoes while he sat reading the paper. Then he'd check himself out in the mirror one last time and walk out slamming the door behind him which was his way of saying "Mind your own goddamned business where I'm going." That is precisely what I wanted to do. Sometimes he'd sit back in the chair looking like a ten-year-old brat with that sneering grin on his face and say "What are you going to do about it then?" He was so arrogant that when I got rid of that tramp with his filth and dirt inside her he didn't care. Far be it for me to say and break her little heart. But broke it probably was and for nothing too. No, he went off his head because I got the better of him. I'd sent a letter to the girl's mother and she sent her packing. If that girl could have seen him when he found out she'd have known what a fool she'd been. That tramp would have been on her bended knees thanking me for what I'd done. I'd have liked that. Kissing my hand in front of him, glorifying me for showing her what he really was. He was so winded that at

first he just looked at me and said "I don't understand you."
Ha! I've given up listening to that. It covers a multitude;
beatings, abuse, the threats of "You've gone too far this time.
I'm goin' to fuckin' kill you." Bowsies aren't hard to come
by. They don't understand you so they beat you so they will.
Then they understand even less so they beat you again.
And again so they will not. It's the perfect excuse for being
a bowsie.

I worry about the east winds blowing in off the sea. Willy's
asthma. Coughs and colds. Alice Turner says I worry too
much but she doesn't have to put up with . . . yes, maybe she
does. But that's her tough luck. What matters is that I have
to. I own nothing. He reminds me often enough. "If it wasn't
for me you'd be out on the streets. Just you remember that,"
he says.

"Lady of the Manor, don't touch that dirty towel. Don't
touch that dirty floor. Here let me pour you a cup of tea."

"Thank you! Thank you!"

"For fucks sake, I'm doing my best. If you don't stop
sneering I'll give you my fist. You've never gone hungry have
you?"

"And where is the rest of it going. On your fancy women,
them tramps you pick up off the streets."

Alice's husband is an alcoholic. I think I'd rather have an
alcoholic than a beater. Preferably none at all. But what
else could I do then or now? The lily was already fading.
There was nothing left. Betty with her shining long red hair
was dead. Long since dead under the clay. I'll teach my Sara
to do better than I did. A rich man or no man, not a bastard
though they all are, but at least have a bit of comfort with it.

I can still see the lily though fainter now, but in the far off
if I squint my eyes and look out anywhere, it doesn't matter
where, I can just about see it. But can it see me? Can it? Can
it? No. Betty with the long red hair. My sister. Haunting
blooms not worth a damn now. When I looked at her I knew
I was meant to be a poet but we weren't thoroughbreds. I
wasn't even sure what a poet was when I got down to it.
Toilet around the back of the house. Remember going out in
the dead of night and feeling my way in the dark. Every spot
of dark was a dead body ready to pounce. It was that or the

chamber pot under the bed. I chose the dead bodies and howling cats through no fault of my own. I hated dirt. "Finicky," I said. "Sickly," Mother said. "Finicky, finicky, finicky," I said. She raised her eyes to heaven and said, "Don't raise your voice to me again." "Finicky," I said, sugary as you like. Betty put orange peels in my bag one time to annoy me. She was sloppy that way. She used the chamber-pot rather than risk the dead bodies. Don't know why she bothered. Always missed, on purpose too I swore. I'd be edgy all night just thinking of the mess. In point of fact I felt so bad about it I'd sneak out to the kitchen for the cloth. Maybe three in the morning and she sleeping like a baby while I fiddled about in the dark with her piss. I brushed her hair every night for her. A hundred strokes. If she was in bad humour she wouldn't let me. "Are you trying to get at me?" "What do you think?" she'd say. Threw everything back at me. Couldn't figure out if she was picking my brains or what. One time I called her from the gate. "Betty come on in. Your dinner's ready." She came running. As I watched her I suddenly sprung back from the gate as though she'd hit me. I started to run off up the road and thinking it was some sort of game she followed me. By the time she caught up on me I was crying. She put her arms around me. "Tell Betty Lee why you're crying," she said. She always called herself Betty Lee, never 'me', or 'Betty'. "Tell Betty Lee. Tell Betty Lee." "Leave me alone," I said and pushed her away. Then I slapped her hard across the face. When Sara was younger I'd pick her up in my arms and pretend she was Betty. "Betty, Betty," I'd whisper. "Where are you now?" Thinking how you can never make the days what they were no matter how hard you try. Not to see her again, the sleeping face and red hair curled about my fingers. Betty Lee. Betty Lee in the foliage of her nineteen summers.

Haunting blooms. Oh! yes, I'd hear her laughter like a high rising wind piercing the quiet land, upturning every hollow and groove and dent with its suddenness. Her face mocking me and then changing into the childish grin as the laughter quivered and flowed along the full red flush of her mouth. And the hot scented smells of summer on her freckled skin and her hair streaming down her back like the reflections of fire through a glass window. Watching her grey eyes restlessly scanning the fields and roads that were so quiet, the sound of her walking beside me echoed through my body like a ghost. And the lilies waving about like white flags through the summer days where I never heard a wind only a soft breeze, barely whispering as I passed by. Feathery, floating, her dress was of rainbow colours. It caught on a bramble as we were climbing through a hole in the hedge. I tried to ease it off without tearing at it. But she was impatient. She tugged at it and tore it free. She kept on running through the long grass shouting for me to chase her. And so I did. So I did. Ring a ring-a-rosy. Betty-is-a-posy. Hasha! Hasha! We-all-fell-down. When he beats me I see violet reflections in the window and the shadows flitting by, armies of shadows of things not coming to pass. Fragile, slender, tripping through the singing grass so lightly you wouldn't have thought it was feet but for the trail of trodden grass left behind by the small neat shapes no bigger than my hand, half-touching the ground. And the echo of laughter. I hear that echo in the swift violet reflections, now here, now there, the gurgle of laughter dying away with the armies of shadows.

My mother. She never forgave me. She pretended she didn't know that while Betty was dying I was already carrying his child. She wished me dead. If she could just have buried me under the same earth the lilies had sprung from and pretended I'd never existed. And Betty laughing at her under the red hair. A golden colour when she was younger, but by the time she was dying it had turned to a dull deep red. The thick hair on the white pillow and mother's lips moving in silent prayer and I thinking, 'Can you see the red against the white? Can you see that?' But her eyes were shut tight praying over her. The same eyes that raked the skin off my body only months before.

"I see you. Don't think I can't see you walking through the door with the bag of groceries." I thought she was trying to let bygones be bygones. But I was wrong. They were a reminder, a constant once-a-week reminder of my lowly place. I'd take no notice of them as she sat by the kitchen table with the bag propped up against the leg of the chair. For all anyone said to her she mightn't have come visiting at all except for the charity she left behind. She left me to bear it all on my own, and I said, "You'll go where the hell is. Hell's fire and all the other trash in your head will soon be waiting for you on your death bed." Soon and not soon enough for me. The fear of it is what counts. It's forced on you on account of the fear. It'll come like balls of fire through your skull the very thing you pray against. But that night when I suddenly thought 'What is is', I found out that what I thought was happening wasn't happening at all and all I had to do was to let him do what he wanted with me and he'd never know.

When I felt the first stirring of his filth and dirt inside me I knew what it was going to do to me. I thought how easy it was for the priests and nuns to preach about motherhood when they didn't have to pay for it. They didn't have to give their whole life to exalt the motherhood they worshipped from the altar of God.

Then I had Sara. And then two more. And I thought how the same 'motherhood' cut through me like a knife as I lay in the dark waiting for them to exalt me while I listened for his footsteps on the stairs knowing how he'd beat me if I refused him. The people who preached that word didn't know the meaning of it. If they lived what they preached they would have found out that motherhood wasn't a thing to be welcomed with open arms but sleepless nights followed by thrashings and beatings that left no place for dignity or reverence or whatever it is they wanted you to believe 'motherhood' was.

So I gave him four children. But I said he would pay for them. He would never pay the way I had to but he would pay as much as he was able. That nourished me and gave me the strength to go on. It was like a beacon of light in the dark nights drawing me closer and closer to the wild churning of my own blood until I was so consumed that the nights ceased to exist and all that mattered was that light. I worked it just right. I lay beside him and I could hear the uneasy silence in him, eating him up as he tried to find the words that would tell him. I gave him what he wanted so he wouldn't find out that it wasn't what he wanted at all. When I'd feel his heavy weight on top of me and his hands fumbling over the dead virgin lands I'd say to him with voiceless words, "You didn't even bother to know I was already dead. You know nothing. You're so busy sinning you don't even know it's not the sinning that matters so much as the suffering you cause to others. You don't even know what sinning is because you've never had to suffer from it." There was something else he didn't know. I made him marry me but I didn't marry him in the way marriage was intended. I didn't share in the blame for the terrible deed inside me. It wasn't of my doing; but once it was done I said I would make him pay. When I told him he'd have to marry me he looked at me in that same bland way I'd mistaken for innocence and later saw as cunning. Cunning in the way every man knows it's not he who will suffer the most. At first he laughed at me. I was three months gone and that was his answer to it! Then he suggested that I get rid of it. Then he tried to trick me. He thought that by not turning up at the church he would shame me into leaving him alone. But I had lost my pride the night he took me. Because I did not consent. I did not. I did not. And so when he didn't turn up the second time I knew that pride was just another word invented by someone who didn't know how life imprisons you. The inventor of that word didn't know that one day was not just more time passing but a relentless tool used by God to remind you that you're already dead in your living. I was there waiting the third time because I knew that every brick and stone and every child was born not from pride but from the guilt of sin.

So I married him to lay me down in the dark nights and hate where no one need ever know with the earth lying over me in the curse of the long relentless hours.

One day I was telling Sara what men were like and she said, "What about me Mammy?" And I said, "What about you?"

Chapter 5

SARA – JANUARY 1965

I remember yes! Sheila O'Sullivan was the first even though I was fatter you could see the difference a mile away her sister came home on hols all glam and told her we should wear corsets otherwise our bellies would fall down by twenty-one. Once Sheila and me were playin' in the school yard and she had it on George Burns came up and kissed her which was a real put down for me eff off she said and started gigglin', I knew the eff off was to tell me she was kissed all the time and was bored by the whole thing and the giggle was to tell him to keep goin' so he did, I could have strangled her so fumigatin' with jealousy was I yes Joseph said my legs were like tree trunks and the smell of sweat off me would knock you flat you're a sweatin' tree trunk he said I started to shout big arse big arse but my lips were like two sail boats bobbin' on water, I couldn't get big arse to come out kept seein' real live arses paradin' around in me head an' I stopped dead. I was a right one all right ma bought me a bra when I started in the tech o fuck you Sheila O'Sullivan I said mine are bigger than yours tech was a great place compared to the national instead of arses mouths became the gobstopper Mr. O'Callaghan taught us Irish he stood behind the girls desks and pulled their bra straps read those verbs out loud ping one day Kathleen stood up and walked out in pure disgust when he did it to her I don't think, then he pulled mine I could feel it pinging against my back like a catapult he bent over me and looked into my exercise book which was empty his hair had a centre partin' with waves sleeked down either side of his head what he didn't know I saw him one night

walkin' along the seafront arm in arm with a woman yes one
girl said she was a widow and he was a widower and they
were goin' to marry his fingers fumblin' again at my back and
his mouth wide open in a grin so sly and knowin' I kept
thinkin' O I have real live breasts like two juicy apples by
then I was sweatin' like a pig and he laughed out loud and
walked up the centre aisle o god the mediterranean ocean
was pourin' out of me armpits yet I knew if me breasts had
fallen off and rolled into the middle of the floor everybody
would laugh and Mr. O'C. would still marry his widow. I
wished I'd stood up and walked out and caused a real
commotion instead. That year was a real commotion in itself
Da havin' that heart attack I nearly died of fright no I didn't
begrudge him his missin' heartbeats one bit my terror was for
meself if he died I'd have to go and work in a factory I'd be
a real nothin' then the dryness behind my eyes and the
tears in front everybody thought I was upset over him he was
like a child no more like a crumpled doll the way he shrank
under the bedclothes I couldn't take my eyes off him so
fascinated by the terror in him and he pleadin' with us to
rally round him and protect him from the death that might
or might not come O big blue eyes shinin' tears after all he'd
done still I was a bit disappointed when he got better I like
things to reach a peak and then explode in front of me eyes,
yes ma was the coolest no nonsense full of common sense O
delicious delicious she had him on his knees for a change
what a thrill and he insured up to the eyeballs as well yes lick
my arse with your martyred face Esther make no mistake
women are stronger than their kitchen sinks wee wee all over
the men when the time comes keep the shit in till the last
minute then pour it down their gobs. Sometimes I got a
terrible urge to put one foot down the toilet an' piss on it to
think of the variations maybe shit all over the new bedspread
on my bed the beach in the middle of all them sun-
worshippers that'd rivet their eyes to the ground for a change
then maybe some night at a dinner dance down it'd come
that stubborn lump catchin' in the hem o' me dress and
plonk onto the floor everyone tryin' to ignore it no doubt O
yes smile sweetly and play footsie with my lump under the
table. Just once I'd like to do it in the chalice any day now

we'll all shit and piss at the same time and flood the world in one go that'll be that O yes singa wingwing all the way to the graveyard.

Boredom is such a killer Ma I'm dead would you please come and feed me to the dogs or else mix me up in cow dung and send me down the country to the farmers as fresh manure. Every night spent lookin' for a boyfriend little men in big jobs and big cars stolen I'd swear that fella Charlie O'Brien do you smoke or drink I asked him all pious and holy a lyin' drunken bastard and he two inches shorter than me still I really put him through the mangle god but I may die roarin' in pain for the insultin' things I said to that fella O to know what it is that makes me want to batter every man to death and afterwards to be so contrite to lie bawlin' in bed and then to start the titterin' like a mad woman's howls what's so funny and not so funny is beyond me the titterin' from me own lips drives me scatty never have I heard such sly devious malingerin' chuckles, you never know yourself it's not beyond the human person to lie roarin' in pain and rollickin' with laughter at the same time. O Charlie O'Brien he kept comin' back for more no doubt he'd a neck like a whale's tooth. Sadie Cummins was the only one I saw fall to bits over the meanderings of love 'tis true then people must wilt and die over each other for a full year which is fifty-two weeks which is 365 days she was loath to even talk about it she bein' sixteen two years older than me she said I wouldn't understand it was all very dramatic to be sittin' in her sittin' room starin' into the fire not sayin' a word but I got bored with the whole business sometimes Rita would join us she's full of understandin' bein' the next best thing to a saint with all her religious ravings she thinks God Almighty is only trottin' after her. I spent me time walkin' from the sittin' room to the kitchen on tiptoe then into the toilet I'd sit down and curse me guts up just for something to do the two of them never heard a word of it so full of will he or will he not come back yes such is the ramifications of my understandin' the same as carbolic soap.

Keenin' keenin' stop your wheenin'
Kiss my arse or Nelly's belly,
Not on your life says Mr. O'Kelly,
Curse and be jasus I'll kiss your arse naked,
Oh yes and pretty cumbersome too
Licky picky where's your micky
Up the yard says Mr. McGrath.

Who knows what O Mr. O'C. I still think of him broke my
heart to leave the tech oh me if only he knew what I was
thinkin' strip him naked in a second scores of others too
O plushy hot lips your guts for garters if the nuns found out
yes sweet little matilda from fairyland innocent eyes to
beguile them all nobody like me cute as a little buttercup the
men won't know what hit them their eyes like fireballs mad
with love for me see them grovellin' all over me but then I
might and I might not all this true love kiss me hand kills
me, everyone says I look real innocent yes blush blush
what's the cure one holy immaculate night in bed with the
lot of them queuin' up waitin' oh now there are other things
besides if only I could think of some it's them bothersome
fellas no wonder I can't I love real oul men O how many arses
have you kissed before mine none of your delicate little
kisses no let's get down to the real business sweatin' like mad
you're about the 100th arse in the last two years Jesus Christ
the excitement of it and not a bit worn out neither rarin' for
more those thick broad shoulders and the trouser belts too
tight around the big bellies me O my I'm a tinker tailor
soldier sailor and the 100th arse no there'd be nothin' like a
bit of experience. I eye every man like mad over forty no
good too feckin' religious afraid of their lives they'll go to
hell I try to give them that wouldn't it be well worth it look
then I give them the long stare like in the pictures full of
know-how and there'll never be another like me not a bit of
good God's curse on it.

Yes Mother Catherine after I finished the national they
started runnin' a club for past pupils killed tellin' us not to
let boys kiss us till we got them up the aisle O humey fraw
I remember well Mother Catherine never said that to me
stuck out like a sore thumb the two of us walkin' them

corridors talkin' about nothin' come with me let's run away
together I wanted to say I didn't the black veil stood in the
way no that's a lie it was her mouth a thing that it was the
lower part shaped like an eel but so soft and fleshy my
fingers itched to touch it and feel it tremble under my
thumbs now to think of it the only reason I went to the club
was for her and she knew O too well she knew sure wasn't
she eggin' me on so safe behind the habit no excuse needed
to go walkin' with me and her hot-flushed face the last time I
never said goodbye just went bringin' her soft mouth with me
there are things you know which is frightenin' because how?
right I will deny them yes too right scared the shit out of me
like lying beside her because I know O my goose pimples
embarrassed yes but not all, much more spread through me is
it true though why not breasts and soft arses and tuft of hair
above the yawning cat all that pink skin like the insides of a
baby's mouth.

Prissoms and pissoms insane with realities Mary dragged
with the Jesus scalp through the graveyard of a double bed
O blood spots on my sheets are you goin' to curse me now
and forever there's a knife in me father's black belly I'll slice
the spit in his mouth with my cutting tongue lie down beside
him succumb at last to the blood from my oozing heart.
Sittin' around waitin' for someone to marry me ma says
when I've kids of me own I'll understand ha too fuckin' well
I will no thank you I'd end up a bloody alcoholic just like
Mr. Turner a real mud rattler god when the saliva starts
drippin' out the side of his mouth I turn green.

Her long slim fingers rough and worn two stained yellow
dirt up the nails what matter I couldn't imagine I kept
thinkin' imagine her what? her a woman that's what it was
the sink escaping, the falling shadows fell on the wooden
cabinet beside instead time is on your side she said suddenly
she didn't look up kept reading the paper after she said it I
thought just a stroke between the two slicing the word
mother down the centre mot-her. She his mot one time I
could kill her for that tears me heart out she must have
been a girl, then a woman not a mot one time. She forgets by
now what it's like, when I first got me period I thought
I'd done it in me knickers I tore up to the toilet to have a

look covered in blood not piss no bloody blood nearly died
on the spot a haemorrhage in the head I pictured meself
dyin' roarin' in pain the wrong end up down I goes like a
little light to her and she blushes and says that's a woman's
thing she gave me a san towel and a bit of elastic out of the
drawer I wasn't sure if she was coddin' me I couldn't walk
proper went around like a duck all day when it hit me what
it was, yes I said his number's up his mockin' jeerin' days are
over I'll see to that this was no big thing with me seein' as
how I covered him up in me dreams every night but in real
life no how'd I get him to step into a big pot of boilin' water.
The thing was when I was left alone I was an out-an-out
toughie there's a streak in me like when I lose me temper I'd
nail anyone to the wall sometimes in school when I'd know I
was headin' for trouble I'd plan the whole thing the day
before word for word like I'd tell the nun I'd scar her for life
if she didn't shut her mouth I often wonder if the nuns kiss
each other if I knew that I'd have them on their knees but
when it comes to the push me nerves went to pieces an me
knees knocked together I had a little flick knife an I'd have
just loved to scoop it around one of their eyes real neat so's
the whole thing would plop onto the floor like a taw. Oh
God I was sick with love for him I could hear it rumblin'
down the sweatin' of me armpits when he was in the kitchen
half-naked and Maggie howlin' when she'd feel the sweat for
him all for him every last drop and God knows no I don't
believe because ma was right so right but I didn't care.

That was when Maggie first started thinkin' it. Thinkin' it.

Chapter 6

SARA – NOVEMBER 1965

She was undressing. The tops of her legs were as skinny as her
ankles. But it wasn't that. They had shrunk. One minute she
was there and the next he was yelling at her. Then I was
running down the hill after her and calling but she wasn't
minding. Running out of the day, behind the mirror where I
couldn't reach her because she was sitting on the bench at
the bottom of the hill still not minding me.

"Are you goin' to run away Mammy? Are you?"

Run out of the day without me? You can't see me. You
can't see me.

"Don't cry Mammy," I said. "Don't cry." But she wasn't.
She was shrunk down to where you can't. It began to drizzle
rain.

"He's thrown you out. How will we run away in the rain
Mammy?" I asked.

And still she wasn't talking. She was staring up at the sky
where she couldn't see the rain. I put my hand on her lap
only she couldn't feel it. So I moved up closer but still she
couldn't. After a while her hair was dripping wet. She got up
and started walking back up the hill. Her apron billowed out
like a balloon in the wind and I started crying. She looked
down at me and said, "Hush. We're going home." And I
said, "Why don't you run away? Why, Mammy, why?" And
she said "Hush" again.

Then she was back in the day and I stopped walking but
the crying wouldn't stop, so I yelled after her, "Why,
Mammy? Why don't you run away?" She walked on ahead
and didn't look back until she turned in the gate. But I

couldn't see if she was looking at me or not because the crying was blinding me.

"Your father is a gambler at heart," Ma said. "That's why he never had a steady job. Always looking for something better. There is nothing better. There is only what we have now and we wouldn't even have that if it wasn't for me. Scrimped and saved, near broke my back to keep food on the table. You want to look out. You have the same streak. You take it from me, it's not the same for a girl. Get some common sense into your head before it's too late. Before some young fella leads you astray, because they do. Believe me, they do. Are you listening to me, Sara? Are you?"

"Leave her alone," Joseph said. "You're always gettin' at her."

"You stay out of this," she said. "It's different for a girl. I only want her to be sensible and save her money. The wardrobe's bulgin' with clothes. She's enough clothes to last her two lifetimes. She should be saving for a deposit on a house. Thinking of the future instead of gadding about all hours of the night."

"But she's not even goin' with anyone. What'd she want to save up for a house when she's got no fella," Joseph said.

"I told you to stay out of this, didn't I? I'll speak to your father about you. Sara, are you listening? What are you staring out the window for? Do I have to repeat myself? Why do you give me all this worry? Haven't I had enough? Am I not entitled to a rest now you're all grown? Of them all you should be giving me the least trouble. Boys are boys. A girl you would think, but no, if it wasn't for Ben, the only one who gives a damn about his mother, I would go off my head because I can't get through to you. You won't listen to me. Now don't interrupt while I'm talking. When do I ever get the chance? You're like a lodger in this house, Miss High and Mighty, who doesn't think her own mother is good enough to listen to. I haven't been outside this house for eighteen years except to go shopping but that doesn't mean I don't know what's going on around me. I only have to look at you to know. That filth and muck on your face is more than enough to tell me you're looking for trouble. You needn't come back here when it happens because the door will be shut in your face. Do you hear me? I'm telling you for your own good. So don't say you haven't been warned."

"What are you talking about?" Joseph said. "She hasn't done anything. Have you, Sara? You're all steamed up about nothing."

"Did I say she had? Did I? You keep out of this. You wouldn't understand what I'm talking about. If it wasn't for Ben I could just curl up and die. He's the only one in this house with any respect for his mother. She won't even tell me where she goes at night. What am I to think?"

"I didn't want to say in front of her," Joseph said. "But she's right. You're an eejit. You ought to be careful. Why don't you tell her where you're going and not be worrying her?"

"If I say where I'm goin' Da will follow me," I said.

"That's rubbish talk. What'd he want to follow you for?"

"How do I know? He just does. He follows me everywhere an' makes a holy show of me."

"How's he do that?"

"You remember the time I had a date with that David fella from Taylor's. We went to the pictures and when we came out he was sittin' in the car waitin' for me."

"Maybe he was just parked there waitin' for someone else," Joseph said.

"No, he wasn't. When David walked me up home he was sittin' outside the house in the car and he rolled the window down and shouted over at me."

"What'd he say?" Joseph asked.

" 'Get into the house you, you crazy little bitch.' And he didn't move outa the car until David was gone. David took off like a light down the road. It was terrible and it's not the first time either."

"Well, maybe he was right," Joseph said. "I remember when you were small you had to be taken away to hospital because you wouldn't stop screaming at night. You were a right fool in them days."

"Leave me alone you," I shouted. "Just leave me alone."

"You're all a shower of gobshites," Da said.
"If you've nothing better to say keep your mouth shut," Ma snapped at him.
"Well they are," he said. "You've often said it yourself."
She dried her hands in her apron and picked the basin up and handed it to me.
"Put them on the line and don't forget to peg the shirts by the tails."
"You know what you are?" she said, turning to him. "You're a bloody antichrist. That's what you are."
When I was finished pegging the washing I went upstairs and lay on their bed. A belly on a belly like sister rose's petals, soft swaying and rocking on the breeze of his last night's sleep. I reach up and press my lips against the window pane. The cold moist glass is unmoved, yet I flow ripple with heat, run my fingers along my lips and I am kissed again. My tongue licks the cold glass, arches itself around the pink skin of my mouth, runs along my teeth. I feel my softness, my roundness. I am stilled by the flow, the currents running through my body. I listen to the reservoir, the beats of my heart, the call of my soul. So softly now I sing, moved by the pleasures of my soaring rhythms. My legs rub against each other. I feel the lushness of my flesh. This is my world. My arms enfold my breasts. My feet touch. We are all one now, absorbed into each other. Swaying, rocking, I curve, arch, reach out and I am still one. Through me, in me, sailing softly on a breeze, my spirit is born again and again. No scar deep enough to wound her, she soars through the nerves of my body, untouched, unbloodied. Her silence like a golden trumpet echoes her triumph as we sway, rock, touch, all in one. Oh! the heather blooms on the hilltops. The sun melting my skin, shiny drops on my forehead, on my cheeks. My whole body lathered in sweat after the long climb uphill. I saw the heather then, so cool outside my perspiring body. And I remembered. I kept the picture of the rolling hills, the long luscious grass amidst the bushes, in my mind. I picked a petal from a rose growing at the side of our

house. Images of myself, delicate as the shades of pink in my palm and wild as the blooming heather.

But then I see Maggie looking down on me. "So is your mother," she screeches. "So is your mother."

"Do you know the facts of life?" Kathleen asked, sitting up on the edge of the desk.

"That's goin' to fall if you keep your weight on it," I said. She bent down, her forehead almost touching against mine.

"Do you know them?" she said.

"Of course, I do," I said. "Now get up off my desk. I want to get my pen."

"The girls say if you tell Father Scott you don't he brings you down to the teacher's room and tells you personally," she said. "And when I say 'personally', I mean personally. They say he goes beetroot."

She swung off my desk and pulled a chair up. "Course if you're not interested in seeing a priest go beetroot over the facts of life, that's okay. I bet you wouldn't have the nerve to ask him."

"Bet I would then," I said. "You put your money where your mouth is an' I'll ask him."

She took a shilling out of her pocket and put it on the desk.

"That says you haven't got the guts to do it."

"Okay," I said. "I'll do it. Give me a week an' I'll empty your pockets for ya."

"You've got 'till Friday," she says, putting the shilling back in her pocket. "Beetroot. You just keep thinkin' 'beetroot'!"

The following morning I went down to the teacher's room and hung around outside until they were gone. The door was open but I knocked and waited for him to say. He was standing by the window.

"Why do you think such a good-lookin' fella becomes a priest?" Kathleen had said.

"Come in," he said, without looking around.

"I was lookin' for you, Father."

"Well. Come in and sit down," he said, turning and pointing to a chair. I sat down.

"What did you want to see me about?" he asked.

"It's . . . . It's about the facts of life, Father," I said.

"Yes. Yes. Go on," he said.

He was beetroot. He was already beetroot.

"Well," I said. "I don't know them, Father."

He walked back over to the window and looked out.

"Didn't your mother ever tell you anything?"

"No, Father. She told me nothin'."

"Meet me here after school, tomorrow," he said.

"Oh! Thank you, Father. Thank you," I said.

I ran up the stairs two at a time and into the toilets. Kathleen was sitting on the window-sill waiting for me. I stood in front of the mirror and started combing my hair.

"Well? Tell us for God's sake," she said. "What happened?"

"You just don't spend that shillin'," I said, " 'cause it's goin' to be mine before long."

The following day I came out of the classroom and met him on the stairs.

"I'll see you in ten minutes," he said and went on down. Kathleen came rushing out of the classroom.

"What'd he say?"

"I've to meet him in ten minutes."

We started laughin' and the other girls came out onto the landing.

"Father Scott is going to tell her," she yelled. "In ten minutes he's goin' to go beetroot. God! I wish I could see him."

I leaned over the banisters and looked down. He was standing at the foot of the stairs, listening to every word.

"Come down here, Miss," he called.

"Christ! Are you in for it, now," Kathleen whispered.

"Go down to the gym hall and wait there until I come," he said.

The hall was empty. I sat on the floor and waited. He came in with a chair and set it down in the middle of the room.

"Sit on that and read this," he thrust a blue-covered book

into my hand.

"Read the first section only," he said. "The second part doesn't concern you."

He stood over by the door while I read it. I couldn't see him go beetroot.

"I'm finished now, Father," I said. "Can I get up?"

He came over and took the book from me and looked down at me.

"Now you know what you already know. Isn't that right, Miss Kavanagh?"

"Yes. That's right, Father," I said.

"Well you may leave now," he said.

It was the going beetroot. As near as possible to the Lord Jesus Christ himself.

Kathleen came running out into the rain.

"Around the back," she said. "My mother has a visitor."

We went down to the shed at the bottom of her garden.

"I'm going to England on the tenth to a boarding school," she said.

"Can't you get a job here?" I asked.

"Don't be silly. My father's rich. He's over in England. Did I tell you that?"

"No. You never said. I thought he was dead."

"Well. Mother doesn't like to talk about him. She says he ran out on her when I was small. Anyway he's paying for the school."

We sat watching the rain dropping onto the leaves in front of the shed and looping and sliding down onto the ground.

"I won't see you any more then?" I said.

"I'll be home on holidays. We can write in between."

"Yes, we can write, anyway. Are you glad you're going?"

She stood up and walked over to the door of the shed.

"It's a great chance, isn't it?" she said.

"Yes, I suppose it is."

"My mother says I'm lucky to get such an opportunity."

"Who's visiting your mother?"

"A friend. A man friend," she said.

"Mr. Ryan then?"

She turned around suddenly. "She goes to bed with him," she said.

"I don't believe you. You're makin' it up."

"She does so. I saw for myself. She sends me down here when he comes. Would you like to see them at it?" she said.

"We couldn't do that. She'd kill us if she found out. Anyway I don't believe you."

"Well, come up and see for yourself, then," she said.

"But that's spyin'. That's a terrible thing to do," I said.

"Well I'm goin' to look. You can stay here if you want to."

I ran up the garden after her.

"What happens if she sees us," I whispered.

"She won't see us. She'll be too busy to look out the window.

We crept up through the garden and around by the side of the house. It was still raining heavily. We peeped in through the bedroom window.

"See, I told you," Kathleen whispered.

They were naked in the bed. Kathleen's mother was smoking a cigarette. His face was turned to hers and he was laughing.

"She always has a cigarette first," Kathleen whispered. We were looking straight in. She only had to glance our way and she'd see us. He leaned over and kissed her breast.

"Come on," I whispered, pulling at her arm. "Let's go back to the shed."

She shrugged me off. "Don't be stupid. It's only startin'."

"I don't want to see anymore. It's not right."

"He buys her things. He bought her the car for Christmas," she whispered. "She wouldn't be bothered with him unless he was loaded. Why do you think she's sending me away to boarding school?"

"I don't care why," I whispered back. "I'm getting out of here."

I ran down the garden and got out through the back hedge. I saw her watching me, then she turned back to the window. All the way home I kept thinking of the smoke curling over Kathleen's mother's head. It was like the steam in our bathroom. I had been lying in the bath watching the steam rising and thinking how Ma would have a fit because I'd closed the window. She said the steam ruined the paint on the walls. I was watching the steam ruining the paint when Da opened the door. It hit against the side of the bath.

"Get out of there. I want to go to the toilet," he said.

"But I'm only after gettin' in," I said.

"Out," he said.

"Well, just let me get dressed."

But he didn't move from the doorway. I jumped out of the bath and wrapped the towel around me.

"Stupid bitch," he said. "Out!" But his mouth was leering at me. The cigarette smoke was curling above her head and his mouth was leering at me.

"He's a Mammy's boy," Willy said.

"Oh, leave him alone for God's sake," Joseph said.

"Go on home, ya cissy," Willy jeered. "Go home to your Mammy."

Ben jumped on him and started hitting him. They rolled onto the ground. Willy rolled out from under him and sat on his chest.

"Give up or I'll beat the stuffin' outa ya," he said.

Ben didn't answer. He kicked his legs wildly in the air trying to unseat Willy but Willy grabbed his arms and moved up further on his chest. He pinned Ben's arms with his knees.

"Come on Willy! Christ, will you leave him be?" Joseph shouted.

Willy got up. "Aw, go on home, ya cissy," he said.

Ben started on down the road. He turned and shouted. "Ya fuckin' bastard, I'll get you for that."

"Cissy wears perfume. Cissy wears perfume," Willy chanted after him.

First I see numbers. Large numbers scrawled on a grey stone wall. The numbers one to four are chalked in a zig-zag pattern because of the unevenness of the stone. The figure One I study more carefully than the others. And then I am the number on the stone wall. The wall is part of a room full

of strangers. I survey each face in turn until I come upon
three familiar figures. I can hear myself say in a loud voice,
"Are you my brothers?" They turn and look across at me
and shrug their shoulders. Then they separate and mingle
with the other people so that the next time I think of them I
remember them as numbers on a stone wall. The group of
strangers forms into a straight line across the breadth of the
room. Now each face is an exact replica of the one beside it.
They start to advance slowly in my direction. They gather
around me and I can hear the silvery shrill sound of their
voices. I am relieved to see the doll-like faces become live
again as I watch their eyes crinkle up in amusement at the
sound of their own laughter. I sit on the floor and when the
first heavy shoe comes crashing down on my face I begin to
laugh. The blood trickles down my face like a river and they
continue to kick and beat me. I suddenly become aware
that each one knows me intimately and I remember to smile.
Through the flow of blood from my mouth my tongue says,
"Let us celebrate our kinship. To flesh and blood. To flesh
and blood."

"I'm in trouble, Sara," Willy said.
   "Are you, Willy? Why?" I said.
   "I lost me job. I haven't told them yet."
   "Sure what's the harm in that? Can't you get another?"
   "They fired me. I didn't go to work all last week and
someone saw me on the strand and told the boss."
   "What'd ya do that for?"
   "I don't know what got into me," he said. "I just wanted
a few days off."

"Sara, wake up. Wake up. Willy's dead. Wake up. He killed
himself. Sara. Wake up."
   It was Ben shaking me. I jumped out of bed and ran in.
Da had him hanging over the bed by the shoulders. He threw
him back down on the bed and beat him around the face. He
kept beating him and throwing him back on the bed and
picking him up again and beating him. I could hear Willy

crying a long way off. Not loud, or even quiet, not in the room or in Willy. But in the distance of a dead sleep.

"What are you doin'," I shouted at Da. "Can't you see he's sick."

"You mind your own fuckin' business."

I ran downstairs. Ma was sitting in the chair with a note in one hand and a cigarette in the other.

"What's Da beatin' the hell outa Willy for?" I asked. She handed me the note. "He took some of your father's pills," she said.

I read the note. "I'm sorry. I can't take anymore. I love you, Mammy and Daddy. Willy."

"A doctor Ma. He needs a doctor," I said. "Da will kill him. You've got to get a doctor."

"Haven't I enough on my plate. Need I remind you of the worries I have to put up with."

"You just go on smokin' your fags," I shouted. "You just do that."

I ran back upstairs. Ben and Joseph were standing in the doorway. Da was leaning over Willy's bed still holding him by the shirt of his pyjamas.

"You little fucker. You stupid little fucker," he shouted at Willy.

Willy was real calm, like he was still far away in the sleep. His eyes were wide open and he was watching us, almost smiling. When Da was gone I went over to him.

"Can you hear me, Willy?" I asked. He shook his head. The quiet of a smile still glimmering in his eyes. That smile was so quiet!

"Are you all right, Willy?" Do you feel sick?"

He turned his face to the wall. "Leave me alone. I'm o.k." he said.

"If it wasn't for me your father wouldn't let you out at all. You know that don't you?" she said.

"Why not. I'm workin' now. I should be allowed."

"I know that. You know that. But your father is another matter. Your father is a funny man and I don't mean funny ha-ha either."

"Well am I allowed out then?"

"Yes but if it wasn't for me. I told him he'd have to let you out sooner or later. 'How is she going to marry, if you don't let her out?' I said. Do you know what he said, Sara? 'Who'd marry that stupid bitch?' That's what he said. You keep that to yourself now, do you hear. I don't want trouble. All I want is for you to have the chance to meet someone."

The door of the church was open. I walked into the stillness, "You do it just right now," Maggie said. The pews were empty but the air was heavy with the prayers of yesterday's voices, flowing down the aisle, relinquishing not one sound or breath. For to pray sweet cry of hope.

The priest had said, "How can I help you if you don't know what's wrong with you?"

"It's them," I told him. "Ma and Da. I can't stand what's going on, Father."

"Well, apart from your father beating you, what is going on?"

"I don't know, Father, but I just can't stand it."

"Well, I'll call to your house some night. You can tell them it's just a social call. It's quite usual."

"I think you must be imagining things," he said. "Your parents seem very nice to me. Try to pull yourself out of these depressions. Try to grow up. You're very immature. Stop looking for attention all the time."

The sweating flesh and the bones kneeling on the pews so I could almost see the heads bent praying over the golden tarnished plaques. 'In commemoration of . . . .' Jesus was here.

I walked up the aisle and knelt at the communion rail. I took out the box of matches and watched the red flames licking the white cloth. Then I stood up and blessed myself and walked back down the sweet cry of hope.

I shut the door of the church after me and went for a walk.

Chapter 7

SARA – APRIL 1966

I lay listening hearing the sleep in the room.

'One day you will wake and they will not.' Hearing the sleep like I could hear what was not said and wonder why, because Ma said, "You can't be told anything." And I said "There is more than one way of saying things and I have listened." Have had to listen because you said 'Who do you think you are wanting a room of your own?' You can't cry and you don't want me to cry because that would be to say . . . . all right then I won't. I will do much worse.

It was late spring and I was deliberately letting the days go by. I got up and went to the bathroom and came back to bed. Da was still asleep but Ma turned over and leaned on one elbow. She squinted at the clock on the dressing-table.

"You'll be late for work, Sara. It's after eight."

"It's Saturday. You know I don't work on Saturdays."

She lay back down and turned to face the wall.

"Where's your mother, then? Where's your mother?" Maggie chuckled. "Sweeping and scrubbing the prison cell. Where was she the last time you saw her. On her knees with that veiled look. 'You can't do anything more to me now. Well, I will do it to myself then.' She bewitches you with the scorching flames of her soul," Maggie whispered. "Your mother is an ocean with trembling waves tumbling and falling back, leaving behind weeping drops that sink fast into the dry sand. And you guard her deserted beach like a soldier while the waves rise up in anger against you, so you could swear you heard her howling at you as she falls on her back. But you knelt to meet her, your hands drifting along with the waves until they were burned with the flames from her scorching soul. Sizzling, burning, burying your bones in the aged flesh of her defiant waters. The flames leapt around your feet and curled around your body. Oh yes, you were so calm then burning away in the crater of her womb, while her flaming sea eagerly licked your flesh and the hot acid roared in your ears. She seduced you with the sound of her silvery bells and flashing shapes. And you said, 'You don't want me,' but you only whispered it. You whispered so you wouldn't even hear yourself saying it. But the ocean heard. The waves quietened, sidled up teasing and caressing your feet. The lapping waters so quiet and still on the whispered words wove and broke and you were forever left suckling or drowning in the waves of your mother the sea. The seaaaaaaaaaaaaaaaaaa," Maggie said.

I could hear the sound of bed springs through the wall. One of them got up and went into the toilet. And then another one. Willy stood in the doorway, his long thin body leaning against the edge of the door.

"Would you say I was a good-lookin' fella, Sara? Would you?" he said.

"It's after nine Ma," he says.

She sits up in the bed. "All right I'll be down in a minute. Put the kettle on will ya?"

He went downstairs. She threw one leg over Da and swung out onto the floor. They fell down years ago. Her back was to me but I could see them dropped at the sides. Mine will too, I thought. Someday I'll look in the mirror and see cow's udders. Where the milk comes dribbling, dribbling. Did ya? Did ya?

I hid myself from her. I wore big loose jumpers so she wouldn't notice my breasts, but her eyes followed me everywhere. Cold hard eyes saying to me, 'I know what you are underneath. I can see through your jumper. I know. I know.' So the day she came into the bedroom when I was undressing I knew what she'd come for. "Let me check your breasts. I want to see if your nipples are turned in like mine," she said. She held my breasts in her hand. She stood in front of me holding them, her eyes boring holes in the wall behind. Then she was gone, without having met my eyes once. Sweating and screaming the no-screams from the hole in my face that was empty. Empty. It wouldn't scream. It wouldn't even try like some rounded idle mouth that didn't know how. When the blood came I said, "I will not. I will not let it come." "Are you, Sara?" she said. And I said. "I will not. I will not." And she said "Are you? Are you, Sara?" And I said, "Can't you hear? Can't you hear what I'm not saying. Can't you Ma. Can't you?" And she said. "You're going to the doctor whether you like it or not. He'll know. Are you, Sara? Tell me." "Can't you hear me Ma? Can't you hear what I'm not saying, like I heard you?"

Last night Maggie was moaning worse than ever. From bed to bed the terrible moaning. A shadow fell darting and flitting between the wardrobe and the dressing-table. Her hair was knotted and tangled and fell about her shoulders like a thick spider's web. The room was ice cold from the chilling moaning sounds. She sat on my bed. "I am eight now," she said. "How old are you and you?" Then her face disappeared but the mocking chuckle beat in and out of my head all night long. All right. All right. I'm thinkin' it.

I could hear them moving about downstairs. Da seemed to be asleep but I couldn't hear the smell so I got dressed under the bedclothes. I went into the bathroom, washed my face and went on down.

"I won't be home for dinner Ma," I say. "I'm goin' to see Gran."

"I hope you're not making a nuisance of yourself going out there every Saturday," she says.

"No. I'm not. I'll be home about eight."

"Well see you don't. People get fed up if you're hanging around their doorsteps all the time."

"She knows I'm coming. I didn't invite meself," I say. Mother of Diviner. When you think. No one to visit her. No one. She'd nearly eat you up for breakfast. Ma talks about Gran as if she was a stranger. Too true.

I got my coat and went out through the front door. Mrs. Turner was cleaning down her steps. She came over and leaned against the wall.

"Good morning, Sara. How's your mother? I haven't seen her in a while," she says.

"Oh, fine, fine. It's a lovely day, isn't it?"

"Yes. Looks like summer is on its way at last. Not before its time," she says.

I imagine the mocking gleam in her eye! But just in case.

"How is Mr. Turner keeping?" I ask.

I swing my shoulder bag along the ground as I walk on down the town and sing, "Mr. Turner is a wino, a wino."

I caught the bus and got out half-way. The roads ahead were empty and dusty. The ditches on both sides were thick with dust. The village was three miles ahead.

A century ago roads with no paths and others walking the same roads, the same dust on the soles of their feet. Funny to think they're dead now. And I walking over the imprints of their feet. Not hearing or moving because they're out of time now like Mary Magdalen and many more with festering sores for hearts.

I walked on, taking my time. The road widened slightly on the bends and swept over the hilly descents like a smooth blast of wind coasting down a mountain. Sores for hearts trooping through the Dead Sea, the mountains, the hills, calling, calling, "Mary Magdalen, wash the dust of the roads off my feet."

If I were to say "Mother and Father". And they were to say "Daughter" and that's all it was. No more. Finished. Finished. Instead of murmuring and weeping into the bones of the past because the mirror was behind her and I saw the long slivering icicles scraping the mirror with the not-tears and the dagger-tipped ends plunging into the marrow of past generations.

She had been waiting all morning. She scrubbed the floor, scrubbed all around him on her hands and knees but she wouldn't ask him to move so she could scrub under the chair. He pretended not to see her. Her nylons were rolled down to her ankles and her face was white with rage. She began again. She hadn't got up off her hands and knees. She crawled over and started again by the back door. When she reached his chair again he was still reading the paper and she scrubbed around him once more. She got up, went over to the sink, emptied the water and refilled the kettle. She lit a cigarette while waiting for the kettle to boil. Trying to find a name for it. Then why don't you tell him if it's just him and not you. She poured the boiling water into the basin and carried it upstairs. I could hear the thumping of the brush on the lino of the stairs. After a while she came back down in her coat and took the shopping-bag off the nail on the kitchen door. She took the duster from under the stairs and began dusting the sideboard. She went into the sitting-room and came back into the kitchen. She looked at the table and went upstairs again. She came back down and sat in the chair with her coat and scarf on. The shopping-bag was by the door where she'd left it. He continued reading. He was smiling behind the paper. Smiling! After a while he put the paper down and took his wallet out of his trouser pocket. He counted eight pound notes and threw them on the table. He picked up the paper again. She took the money and mumbled something. He looked up.

"Did you say something?"

"No. I said nothing."

I found the photograph between the leaves of an old missal. I sat in front of the dressing-table and faced it into the mirror, but I couldn't tell one way or the other. It became a habit, I'd put it away and swear I wouldn't look again but the following day I would. One night I went to see Sadie with the square shape in my pocket mocking the high rising fear. I took it out and handed it to her.

"Guess who that is?" I said.

She looked at it for a minute and went to hand it back.

"Is it your mother when she was young?" she asked.

"Yes. Look properly at it. Who does she remind you of?"

She looked again. "I don't know. Is it supposed to remind me of someone?"

"Doesn't it remind you of, say, Willy?"

"I suppose so. I'm not much good at tellin' though."

"Sadie, look real careful. Would you say I was like her at all?"

"A bit. You'd know she was your mother, like."

"How do you mean a bit? What bit is like her?"

"All over. I mean you'd just know," she said.

I walked down as far as the beach. It was still in my pocket. The mock coming out of the night. On her breath. Out of the same face.

"I want to talk to you. Is that asking too much? Don't I deserve that you would talk to me? Do I have to remind you? No. Well you'll know soon enough. When it's too late. Believe me your mother knows what's best for you. I want to see you settled down, not falling into the same trap as I did. No! I don't mean that. Of course you'll marry. It's different for a boy. What I meant was you make sure, whoever he is, that he's got plenty of money. I'd hate to see you going hungry. What are you talking about, Sara? You're terrible foolish at times. You're still young. That kind of foolish talk will wear outa you. All I'm saying is the important thing is a good job. Let me tell you because I know. Your mother knows. If he's no money he's no good to you. Sara, are you listening to me at all? God, you're an antichrist. You're just like your father."

Out of the night on the cool wind the mock, feeling the face in my pocket. How terrible it is to know that. To look like her. Not old before her time, but shrunk inside herself and then outside until I can't see anything but the dull dead eyes and I not able to say "It's all right," anymore because the night filled up the room with the waiting and the terrible dark. One minute the four feet space was there and then it wasn't.

She's my mother, I thought. She should die for me. Yes, my mother, she should do that. Feeling the face lying in my pocket. It wasn't a photograph by then it was her smiling in the dip of my coat. Not saying anything. Not having to because she was my mother.

Upon the fading day, saying I have walked here and here and here on the wake of your roads and the silvery grey threads of your hair. The light of past generations of mother and daughter, mother and daughter, then daughter and mother, when it was just you and me, me and you. I wish I knew what a mother was. I wish I knew. Because I said, "You should die for me" and you said, "When you have your own you'll understand." Will I? Not "Me. Me. Me," but "Mother. Mother. Mother." And not even knowing that.

He came up the stairs and into the room.

"Get down the stairs and make us supper," he said.

She sat up in the bed her face white and tired, her eyes blinking in the sudden glare of the light.

"I'm not coming," she said. "The doctor says I've to get plenty of rest."

He leaned over the bottom of the bed. "If you're not down in ten minutes," he said, "I'll come up and drag you down by the head of hair."

She put her hands behind her head and lay back against the pillow.

"You'd better go down Mammy," I said. "He'll kill you if you don't."

"Go back to sleep you," she said.

She lay there for a while and I said "Please, Mammy. He'll make a show of ya in front of them men."

She didn't answer but she got up and dressed. Her face was so drawn and I was crying inside for her. I heard her on the stairs and then in the kitchen. The men's voices got louder and louder. Then Maggie came on the wall. She began to moan the long steady howling wail, not stopping to breathe even. The sound raging through the night, an unbroken howling wail, weaving its lonely passage down the years.

After she made supper she came back upstairs and got undressed in the dark.

"Are you all right, Mammy?" I asked.

She didn't answer me. She curled up on her side and faced the wall. I could see her eyes, her dark brown eyes, disbelieving the suffering that's too terrible until it's not suffering but a kind of relief to know you can't feel it anymore. It can go on and on and you hardly know it's there unless it stops.

When he thrashed me she watched with that half-pleased glazed look. Not able to look away and a kind of look on her face, as if to say, "I have found out that the thinking of something being terrible is what makes it terrible. But if you live with it a long time you find it's the same as eating and drinking. Not terrible at all, but a part of the everyday living you have to put up with."

It was after twelve when I reached the village. I walked down to the harbour and stood against the railings and watched a man pulling an empty fish-net onto the stones. He was stripped to the waist. He sat down beside the net and pulled a pipe and matches out of his trouser pocket. Striking a match, he cupped the flames in his hands while he brought it up slowly to the pipe in his mouth. Then he sucked hard and blew out a thin cloud of smoke.

Reminds me of someone. Everybody does. For the life of me I can't remember. Names too. For instance. Percy. Cyril. Banjaxed at your christening. O humey fraw! That was queer.

"My Mammy is dead," Sadie said. She wasn't crying. She stood in the doorway blocking my view.

"You can't come in," she said. "All the relations are here." I doubled up on the step laughing. When she slammed the door in my face I was still laughing.

"He rose again on the third day," the priest said.

"You ought to be ashamed of yourself," Rita said. "She told me you laughed at her."

"My mother's breasts are down to her waist," I said. "I swear. I saw them."

"What are you talking about?" Rita shouted.

"Sadie's mother is dead and my mother's fell down like bird's droppings. And she said 'When you're married you'll know all about it.' Christ was crucified and he rose again, but my mother didn't."

"In God's name what are you saying!" Rita shouted. "You laughed into Sadie's face."

"Hear the smell of sleep in the lick of a second," Maggie said. "Profound and deadly lick of a second from the sleeping mouths and the lids of their eyes sucked down on the dark's indomitable silence. Indomitable but not impenetrable because the drop of his seed was already living, lying not four feet away listening and watching their sleep for the past years. In one night hearing not just eight hours sleep but all the eight-hours sleep and the not-sleep behind their sucked down lids. Forcibly drawn into the four feet space between by the sheer power of that drop of seed that wet the womb. So that the seed could have said at any time, she is thinking this now, or he is thinking that, and she would be right because by her very presence she was safeguarding the silence and so she had to listen to know what it was she was safeguarding. When I found out what they wanted of me," Maggie said. "I knew it would not go away. As long as I lived I would not be able to forget that profound and deadly lick of a second."

I climbed over the wall and walked down onto the stones. The man lying beside the empty fish-net turned and nodded his head in greeting. It was after one. I was beginning to feel hungry. I watched the waves breaking on the edge of the shore. The sky was clouding over in small uneven patches. Gulls were settling on the half-built wall enclosing the harbour.

"You'd think they'd have finished building it." "Half-done did the job just as well." Start to finish. Half-done.

I came back up onto the roadway and crossed over to the café facing the harbour and sat down by the window. The gulls were diving off the half-built wall and sweeping down over the sea searching for food. I could hear their high-pitched screams as they rose one by one into the air. They circled low over the harbour then they climbed higher. They disappeared out of sight. A low-sized woman came around the counter to me.

"What'll it be?" she asks.

"Tea and a sandwich, please."

The café was so small I couldn't imagine it being able to hold enough people to make it worthwhile. As if she was reading my mind the woman leaned on the counter and said "Won't be long now. Not many around here this time of the year, but we do well on the fish-and-chips. Queues down the road sometimes for our fish-and-chips." She brought the tea and sandwich over to me. The tea spilt onto the saucer as she set it down on the table.

"Mind you," she says, "It's still hard to keep the place going. Are you Mrs. Lee's granddaughter then?"

"That's right," I say. "How'd you know that?"

"Sure, wasn't your mother and me at school together. I'd know you out of her anywhere. You tell her Maureen Connolly was asking for her. That's my maiden name. She'll remember me."

"I'll tell her," I say.

I finished the tea and sandwich and walked around by the harbour and on up to the village. I passed Kathleen's house. Is she at it right this minute in the square of the window with the curling smoke curling above their naked bodies? When the smell is gone. Her husband's an architect. Rich. They give her presents like the three wise men coming down the mountains. The gobbos!

Kathleen never once wrote. She said she would but she didn't. I thought it was because she'd be educated and I wouldn't. "I hope she drops dead for not writing," I said. Then I felt real sad because she'd been my best friend. "I hope she has an accident instead of dropping dead," I said. Crippled and educated. That was queer to think.

"Are you thinkin' it," Maggie asked. "All right, I'm

thinkin' it," I said. "The silence of the not-spoken words where the tears were myriad and wanting," Maggie said. 'Thinking them is enough,' I thought but they weren't of thinking at all. When next I saw them they were hard, not crisp but rock-like in their putrid hate. Crackling through the long and lonely bones of her wrinkled face. Waiting in her grave for her, her grave not even dug yet but already laid out through the not-words. The not-crying. And I thinking Mama, Mama, the first gurgling drops of spit and breathless longing. She was gone as far back as that. She could not hear the first weeping drops that went into the making of the light rays. So too with the not-tears. They were lying in the grave not even dug.

I walked up to the crossroads and turned into the road Gran lived on. I slowed down. I could see Gran sitting in front of the fire. When Grandad died Ma didn't go down to see Gran once the funeral was over. There was no talk about it. It was as if Gran had died too. When I'd come back from visiting Gran, Ma wouldn't mention her. Then a few days later she'd ask how she was and that would be that. I was thirteen when Grandad died. Sometimes I'd think of how terrible it must be for her all on her own and then I'd forget about it. I began taking the bus out and walking down around the harbour and on up to her house. I'd stand outside hoping she might come out and call me in. The curtains were already drawn. I thought she was dead after all. Maybe she died after Grandad's funeral and if I went in I'd find a skeleton in the chair. After about six weeks of coming down and hanging around the gate and going back home again I decided to go in. After that I came every week.

It was nearly three when I reached the house. The gate was loose on the hinges. It lay awkwardly against the hedge, set at an angle. Branches swept down over the pathway forming an arch right up to the front door. I knocked and waited. The walls were covered in creeper. In the summer the tendrils curled in around the hallway. I could hear her heavy footsteps coming down the hall. She opened the door a fraction at first, then wider.

"Oh, it's you. I wasn't expecting you."

She always said that even though I'd come every week. She turned and walked down the hallway into the sitting-room. "Close the door after you."

I closed it and followed her into the sitting-room. She sat in the armchair in front of the blazing fire.

"Pull a chair up," she says. "I'll be glad when there's no more need of a fire. I'm not able to be carrying the coal bucket around from the shed."

I jump up. "Do you want me to get you some?" I say.

"Now sit down. I've enough to be going on with," she says. "I'm glad you've come. Haven't seen a soul all week. I don't like to say, you being her daughter an' all, but your mother's a cruel woman."

She started on and on about Ma. Every week the same oul thing. And then when I'd be leaving she'd say, "Well I've had my say now. I'll never mention her again."

"I hear she doesn't go to Mass," she says. "Is that true?"

"Well I don't know," I say. "She might and I wouldn't know. There's the Mass in the evenings now. I'd be out."

"Aye. That's right, you'd defend her. I wouldn't want to put you against your mother but if she loses her religion she's done for. We all grow old, you know. She forgets that. Someday it'll be her turn whether she likes it or not. Then she'll know how important your religion is. The priest was here last week," she says. "He wanted to know if I'd like the communion brought to me instead of going to Mass. I told him as long as I was able I'd go to the church. He said I was a great woman. Your mother doesn't know that. He asked me if I ever had visitors. I told him the truth. I told him my daughter never visited me. All the neighbours know she doesn't come. Not that I'd ever say, but they know."

"She gets colds easily," I say. "She seldom goes out."

"That's right, you'd defend her. I wouldn't turn you against her for the world. She's had a hard life. No one knows better than I do. She hadn't a stick of furniture when she moved into that house. I gave her everything. Everything. That's why I can't understand why she leaves me like this. I pray to God she'll come to her senses soon."

She gets up and goes over to the kettle.

"Here, let me," I say. "You sit down an' I'll make the tea."

"You stay where you are," she says.

She stopped talking, but her voice lingered in the room like the ticking of a clock, persistent, endless, reverberating through the day as if waiting for her to say "You may leave the room now." We had tea and biscuits. She talked again about Ma. She couldn't stop repeating the same things over and over again. In some ways she frightened me, but not Maggie. I could hear Maggie laughing at her. At six o'clock I got up to go. She walked down to the gate with me.

"I'm sure you're sick listening to me," she says. "Well, I've had my say now. I won't mention it again. You'll be coming next Saturday?"

"Yes," I say. "I'll be here around the same time."

Half-way down the road I turned and waved to her. I felt sorry for her then. I'd have liked to have gone back and given her a hug but I knew she couldn't bear it. I remember last Christmas I bought her a present and she seemed so pleased I put my arms around her, but she pushed me away.

I missed the bus and thought about going down to the station for a train. I decided against it. The sun was slanting low over the houses. I felt it stirring in my belly and then gurgling up to my throat. I began to laugh. I howled with laughter. I couldn't stop it, winding and thrusting knots out of the fear of crying. I sat down on a grass verge on the side of the road and watched the cars going by. I felt cold. I could feel the evening breeze beginning to chill my face. A woman went by on the opposite side of the road. She looked over. Only tinkers sit on grass and footpaths. "Mag Mag the tinker's rag."

I got up off the grass verge and began walking home. I could sleep thinking of it. But I wasn't thinking anymore. Maggie lying in the dust of the road. Over the graves of silent others. Trampled over. Raging and hating in the child of . . . . Done. Finished. All right. All right. Because I have loved you. To see you in the colours, washing through the skin and pouring down onto my face. For me. For me. So I woke up this morning thinking, 'I am just thinkin' it, that's all.' But I wasn't. I was going to, anyway. I was letting the day go by. Christ! Oh yes that man is my father. Your seed said that standing on the face of the earth. How if it was just a man, any man, it would not be all right but it would not be so terrible as to have to say "My Father". Even after all she told me about men. Christ! Oh! yes. She told me but I'd just keep on thinking, 'Oh my father, my father, because I loved you more than anything else in the world. That's why I wasn't bothering to think it. I was just letting you wait.'

I walked the six miles home without even feeling or knowing I was walking. A bus passed me by on the way and slowed down but I waved it on. I must have, though I can't remember. I remember it slowing down a few yards ahead of me and then without its seeming to gather speed the dust flew up from under the wheels and into my face.

It was after nine when I got home. Ma was sitting in the kitchen reading the paper. "Did you have anything to eat?"

"No. I'll put the kettle on and make a cup of tea," I say. "Do you want one?"

"No. I'm not long after my dinner."

I made the tea and sat drinking. She was still reading the paper when I went to bed.

"The carnival isn't coming anymore," she said. "Your father was only renting the field. He has to make money somehow. But it was a dead loss, so that's the end of it."

"It might next year," I said.

"It might not either," she said. "What would we live on in the meantime. Fresh air? As you well know, fresh air is not much good to a starving stomach."

The carnival was gone. That's all I could think of. There were no colours in the winter but I kept saying it's all right. It's all right. The colours will come back when the carnival comes. After she told me it was gone for good I walked down as far as the field. He was leaning over the wall staring at the withered yellow patches of grass.

"What do you want?" he said.

"Ma told me about the carnival."

"Yes," he said. "The people of this town won't support anything."

I leaned over the wall beside him. "Are you sorry to see it go?"

"Yes. I don't know what to do now." And I, "I loved the carnival." And he, "How old are you now." And I, "Almost fourteen." You is my life. And he, "Oh, now is that so?" And I, "Yes, that is so." And he, "Your mother puzzles me sometimes," And I, "Oh." Here I am with you like touching the silky leaves of a daffodil. Let's hold hands and climb a hill together. To sit on the edge of the world and look on with you. And he, "I don't understand her. She hasn't an ounce of feeling in her bones." And I, "Yes, I know." Buy and sell my own mother down the swannee to lean over the wall like this with you. And he, "She's so cold. I can't figure it out." And I, "Well she's had it hard, it isn't easy at all." And he, "No, I don't say I'm an easy man to live with." And I, Let me travel all over your face with my hands. Cool hands all over the face of the earth. And he, "Well you'll be working soon and it won't matter. I'll have done my bit." And I, "Yes." Just hold me tight and let me drown in your colours. Lick your eyelids and kiss away the beads of sweat. O sweet nits of jewels and sweat and bones knocking together in the sweet cool soft of your belly. And he, "How old did you say?" And I, "Almost fourteen, in three months." And he, "You've grown without my noticing. It all comes so fast." And I, in the stillness between us I become music. Sound that enters the tissues of enraptured minds. And he, "I don't like talkin' about your mother, but she worries me." And I, She's an oul' bags. Now, let me take your hand and we'll run away and never come back.

I will not. I will not. And he will not. "I have sinned, Maggie," I said. "Not to God but to my own self." Why? Just tell me why and no more through the dull dead brown eyes. No. Because that would be to say . . . .

The dark came. I could hear her deep breathing four feet away, unhurried and tranquil, diminishing through the pervading whispers where the voice was calling me, sweating and screaming the no-screams. When the house became quite still I got out of the bed and walked on the shadows of my crying down the stairs. I opened the kitchen door. He did not stir in the sleep of his own darkness. I walked over to the cooker and turned the knob on. I heard the gas hissing but he did not stir. I waited until I could smell it in the room. Then I walked back upstairs on the shadows of my crying and lay beneath the cool clean sheets.

"Maggie, I don't hate being a woman," I say. "I don't. I don't."

Chapter 8

MAGGIE – FEBRUARY 1970

In the morning pale bubbles of light infiltrated the closing night and spread through the broken threads of the stretched veil. A steady drizzle of rain fell on the outside world and single drops clung to the window. Clouds gathered in the sky and curled and drifted over the rooftops like a column of sleepwalkers.

Esther rose on one arm and pulled the half-open curtains aside to look out. She looked over at the clock on the mantelpiece before lying down again. It was a quarter-past six.

At exactly seven o'clock she pushed the blankets aside and stepped onto the cold floor. She went into the bathroom and on her way back she knocked on the door of the other bedroom and called out, "It's after seven," before stepping back into the room. She was a small woman, but the fat of her stomach dropped clumsily, lacking muscle and tissue to hold it in shape. Her breasts swung loosely as she lifted the nightdress over her head. They, too, looked as if they had been discarded by the rest of her body, as though the skeleton of the woman had no use for them. When she finished dressing she hit the wooden rail on Sara's bed as she went past.

"Get up, it's after seven," she called.

Sara's eyes were already half-open. She closed them blinking a few times before leaving them open. Esther went downstairs and into the kitchen. After a few minutes she called up, "Will you get up for God's sake."

"All right I'm comin'," Sara replied.

"And call the boys," she said.

Sara looked out the window. The sky was now a dull white and clouds lay flat and motionless against it. She could hear the sound of cars going past and a dog barking. A man whistled and the dog came galloping down the hill.

"Am I going to have trouble this morning of all mornings," Esther called again from the hallway. Her voice was toneless, without emphasis on any of the words as though she didn't require an answer but was listening for the sounds that would confirm the worry in her words. Sara got up and looked over at the empty bed beside her. She went out onto the landing and looked into the other bedroom.

"You'd better get up. She's going mad down there," she said.

Willy leaned his head up against the headboard. "What time is it?"

"It's well after seven. Come on. She's makin' the breakfast."

Presently sounds could be heard all over the house. Esther put the kettle on the gas and lit a cigarette.

"Get the cups and plates out. Make yourself useful," she said to Sara. Willy held a cup of tea in one hand while he searched his pocket with the other.

"I couldn't eat a thing," he said, as he opened his packet of cigarettes.

"They're bad for you with that chest of yours," Esther said.

"I hope the rain stops soon," he said, ignoring her.

"What time are the cars comin' to collect us?" Joseph asked.

"Ten o'clock," Esther said. "The Mass is at half-past."

They spoke without haste, each one listening to the emptiness in the kitchen penetrating their eardrums. The air was a quicksand swallowing up their voices quietly and effortlessly, leaving the emptiness as timeless and powerful as it had been. Because you could feel him in each one of them, their eyes hastily avoiding each other's as they talked. Yet no one spoke about him. It was as if they silently said, "We'll say no more about it now. We won't cry."

"It's early," Sara said. "We shouldn't have got up so early.

I'm going for a walk to pass the time."

"How can you go walking on the day of your father's funeral?" Esther said. "It's not right."

"What's right, then? Should I just sit here for the next two hours waiting for the cars?"

"You shouldn't be seen out," she said.

"I'm going. I won't be long," she said.

"Are you afraid of the shadows, Sara," I asked.

I watched the shadows coming with the night and spreading over the furniture and walls. The night's light streamed in through the window, highlighting the shapes and sizes of the shadows. As I waited for Night's City to come I watched the trapped rage scuttling along the ceiling and floor. The shadows began to take shape, they towered and loomed larger than the house itself. I stood on the landing my hands touching the folds of my skin. The shadows closed in around my naked body and I watched the skin float off in small feather shapes. An older woman stepped out of the shadows at the bottom of the stairs with a basin of water and a scrubbing brush. When she reached the top step she placed the basin of steaming hot water beside me. The steam rose up around me and my flesh peeled off in layers and fell into the basin. Chunks of skin floated around on top of the water like large suds of detergent. She began scrubbing the top step in quick circular movements. She moved slowly downwards, scrubbing with the circular motion until the lino was a glossy shining surface. My bones were completely bare and I began to shake in the icy draught from the open window. The wheeze from my lungs, like a thin shrill whistle, moved downwards with the woman. Occasionally she sat back on her haunches to admire the glow on the worn lino. When she reached the bottom step she looked up at my shivering flesh-less body and lingered for a moment, entranced with the fading light dancing on the yellow-patterned wallpaper behind me. She stepped back into the shadows and the basin lay like a hypnotic eye on the bottom step. It became imperative that I should retrieve the remaining flesh from the basin, but as I started down the stairs the staircase faded and

I could only watch my flesh drowning in the water.

I turned and walked into the bedroom and lay down on a narrow bed against the inner wall. In the double bed opposite me lay a man. He stretched his arm out into the space between us. I reached over and slipped my hand into his. I could barely see his outlined shape in the darkness but I dreamt of the deep furrows in his forehead and the glowing beads of sweat on his soft cheeks. I thought of his mouth, of my mouth, of his mouth and of my mouth. Quite suddenly the older woman appeared on his opposite side. A thick grey mist spiralled around the room. The silence descended from the ceiling and covered my whole body with a smothering despair. The walls and furniture began to fade, receding into a vast distance until there was nothing left but the two beds. The woman sat up and the flesh began to melt off her bones and fall onto the eiderdown like soggy crusts of bread. When I looked down at my own body I saw that it was my flesh that was peeling. I ate the crumbling flesh off the eiderdown like a cat. Then the woman moved her body in circles as she had done with the scrubbing brush until she was blotted out by the enfolding mist.

I lay beside the man but, at the same time, I was still lying on the narrow bed holding his outstretched hand. I put my arm around his shoulder before leaning over to bite deeply into his neck. A waterfall of blood spurted out. It gushed down the side of his neck and onto the sheets. I continued to chew and pull at his flesh, tearing it savagely away from the milky white bones until only his soft moist mouth remained. It pumped and throbbed with blood. I licked it gently from side to side teasing its pulsating fear as it turned purple with terror. Then I bit into the middle of it, a sharp clean even bite, before swallowing his whole mouth. I sat back on the soft white pillow and watched his bones slipping and sliding, until they were sucked under by the thick bog of blood on the bed. I lay back on my own narrow bed chuckling to myself as I licked the last crumbs of flesh from around my mouth.

I wouldn't forgive Sara for still loving him after what he'd done to me. I warned her I wasn't one to be cast aside lightly and ignored by anyone, especially not by her who was fool enough to go on loving him without reckoning on me. So when the last sounds struck no chord in the sleep of the house the contours of the room faded into the fallen dark and revealed the City of Night.

We went downstairs and into the kitchen. He was asleep when we opened the door and went over and turned the gas on full. We came back upstairs and I lay awake remembering my hoarse cries when I saw the first flow of blood trickling down my legs and spattering the edge of the toilet bowl. "If he had mutilated me," I said. "Scarred me, it would have been far better than this red-rimmed cursed open sea of me." Then I thought of the gas filling the kitchen and I slept peacefully for the first time in eight years.

The next morning when Sara woke up and found him asleep in bed she cried with relief. "I did what you wanted, Maggie," she said. "Now leave me alone." "You did nothing," I said. "Nothing but cause trouble."

So he had woken up in time, the cunning bastard, but he never mentioned what we'd done to anyone. I knew then I had had my revenge. I knew he had not forgotten those nights, any more than I had. It wasn't one of his sly secrets he could bury under Night's City. He was afraid to accuse me because he would then have had to pay the price of my death.

For the four years since, he was dead to me. I watched his spirit die away inside him and I said, "Good enough for you. What would you know? What would you or any man know?" Yesterday he shut his eyes forever, but still the dark came. It stretched from wall to wall as if an unseen hand was covering the sleep in the room with a veil so as to protect its final hours. But I did not sleep: the snake came. He slithered along the ceiling. His tongue slipped in and out of his mouth. His small round eyes watched me. He slid up fast inside me, then slow. I am going back now. To the valley bowed down with heavy branches. I walk through long grass. Cloudless blue sky shelters me. Snake is curled up inside me. He sleeps now, contented, so full of ecstasy. I smile, feel so light of body with him in me. But then I begin to grow small. Am so minute. Feel so angry as the world grows on without me. The grass grows taller. Green swishing blades murmur to the trees. The trees, gnarled and old, bow to the winds. Autumn comes, and I hear the leaves on trees go crisp and fall from the branches. Rain washes over me. Light of day flashes past. Then darkness descends. And all the seasons circle around me and howl at my minute form. Now I feel the serpent move. Head alert. Swinging tail stings me. I can see through my womb. His skin crawls with fear. Prickly to my flesh. Womb grows cold, tightens up. Snake turns and dives between my legs. Then disappears through the long grass. I grow smaller and smaller. I cannot feel myself. I cannot feel myself, I moan and the waves sweep into the air like curled silver-edged blades under the dark sky.

When Sara went to school each day with her satchel on her back I was really at home. The nun sat at the top of the classroom, her long veil flowing about her face.

A hair escaped from the habit and curled about her ear. I saw her in a dress of pink and white that flattered the smooth roundness of her shoulders. I laid my head against her soft pillow and touched her to find she was a woman. This made me happy. Her mother, her sister, her daughter, we lay together. Beside us sat a girl with nits in her hair. To whom should I have told my secrets? To this nit-ridden head poring over her copy book. Anxious and guilty, the blank sheets became the scaffolding from which she would hang. As she shook her head the nits flashed like jewels in the sun. Then a halo around her head. She swung like a pendulum as the white sheets became blanker and blanker. Which was more terrifying for her, her empty copy book or the slender nun who looked over her shoulder? "Little to be gained by having nothing to say," the nun said. Sara's own pen slid across and down her page but I continued to paint in my head until my head was full and my copybook, too, was blank.

I've passed by faces and faces have passed me by. I see them all with the headscarves tied tight under their chins. So tight, as if the knot is holding the head onto the shoulders. They walk past, dark swollen hunched shapes. I see them coming down the hill. There could be six or sixty for all I can tell. They could come closer together and give each other protection against the wind and rain but they don't, they walk far apart. When they reach the bottom of the hill they turn around and begin the steep climb upwards. I step out and call up to them. "Which one of you bitches is my mother? Come on. Which one?" They stop walking and take off their headscarves. Everyone of them has her face. So that there may be six or sixty on that hill and every one of them is she. They come down to me and when they are near enough one screams, "Are you accusing me of being your mother?" "Yes," I say. "I'm accusing you, just like you accused me."

Sara walked up the back roads out of the town and by the time she got back the funeral cars were outside the house. She sat in the car beside Esther. Esther shrank back into the corner of the seat as Sara's arm touched against hers.

By the time we reached the church quite a crowd of people had gathered around the door. We sat together in the front row. Sara sat on the right hand side of Esther and the boys on the other.

The boys, oh yes the boys! And where are my brothers? Look at Ben, he is a clown. Flitting in and out of the days with lustrous shining eyes and nimble feet. He pirouettes around the kitchen. Is he here at all? Then he hears music and his mood changes. His body gyrates and twists. And his feet, like sun flashing off the blade of a knife, skim the floor, the ceiling, the walls. Wings flying alone. Esther tells him to wear his coat on the chilly winter days. But he laughs and leaves it hanging on the door. Then he says he will be a singer. Oh! the bellows of him through the house. This dwarf is so tall, he towers over us all. "I am the youngest," he says. "Leave me out of all this. I will caress your cheeks with the freshness of my youth. I will be your daydreams, your fleeting thoughts. See now I crouch on the floor and push my back up into a hump to become the pinnacle of the mountain you wish to climb." Ah! so innocent. To ask of us in return. "Do not touch my body with your leprous sores. Or pierce my heart with arrows from your envious eyes." How he went on that clown!

And Willy watches him. Puny, delicate Willy who would soon demand his own attention from us all. I can hear his bones scraping together under the thin layer of flesh. I can count them now as he lies in bed gasping for air. They jump and knead under his white skin like twigs under feet. He is a goldfish in an empty bowl. His mouth and nostrils are so wide and open. His eyes stare blankly ahead then roll around like marbles in his sockets as the air tantalizes him with its abundance. His lungs flap up and down. And as we breathe so easily he smothers in a spasm of wheeze and cough. He escapes the heavy hand of his father who is swollen with pity for him. He sinks his teeth into a juicy bone with the gushes of love from his mother. He waves his sickness like a white flag as they both forget to war and pour their love, fraying at the edges like an old teacloth, into his wretched breathless body. He appears to bloom with this new enchantment. But then he wilts away in a new sickness. For he sees that it's his illness that is loved. "But what of Willy?" he asks, lying there in the coffin he has built around himself. "What of Willy?"

Joseph watches both Ben and Willy and knows he is the eldest. This is inescapable. He cannot clown about or be sick. He is so heavy with the weight of his age. So sodden with reality. I see through the veil of my fantasies as he takes reality in the palm of his hand and sifts through its contents.

But where are my brothers now? The clown is gone. Sad doleful eyes follow the figure of his mother around the house. She feeds off her son. And in a way he is loved. He has a new act now, in the privacy of the bathroom. He turns the water on in the bath, then kneels on the floor and puts one shaking hand under the running tap. The water runs down his hands and through his fingers. He reaches over to the ledge for his soap and nailbrush and scrubs the long slim fingers and finely shaped nails until they turn red from the hard bristle. He dries them and holds them up to the light for examination. His eyes hungrily explore the clean flesh. And his whole body tingles with pleasure. He is happier and calmer than he has been all day.

And to the puny delicate creature who gasps for air? He is still gasping and he disguises his body with arrogance.

And the eldest, "I am like my father now," he says. But that is all.

The coffin was only six inches away from me. I could see his full body stretched out and his waxen face turned slowly towards me. His mouth tightened and turned into a leering grin. After the service everyone stood around the church-yard. People came from all directions and pumped Sara's hand up and down.

The funeral passed through the Main Street, slowing the traffic down to a crawl. People stood on the footpaths and stared at the passing coffin. They blessed themselves and raised their eyes to Heaven. Death rattled and was wheeled onto the streets and everyone saluted and bowed to Him.

Oh such a carnival. People screaming with pleasure, the swings rocking in the air. Sara running in and out of the dodgems. Then lying in the corner at the end of the field chewing grass and watching the coloured flags waving in the air. The splendour of the carnival.

She did not answer me. He laughed and my brothers did not know. "Who am I?" That was all I asked. Stretched out lazily in the sky was a rainbow. Soft delicate shades of orange, blue and violet. I lowered my eyes to the grey concrete that surrounded me, then looked up at the sky again. I wished I was a bird. I am ten. Oh! How I ache for smiling. A cheerful smile they said. "Who were they? Who were they?"

"If I hold your hand will you stay with me?" I begged. But she went and he said it was forever. I followed her forever to the wooden bench at the bottom of the hill. This woman who still had her apron on ignored my hand in her lap so I went back under Grandad's apple trees . . . . "I am five now,"

I said. "How old are you? And you?" This is my paradise
under Grandad's apple trees. White-winged doves settle on
the branches and their droppings land on my head. But I
will not move because I was here first. The soldiers are
coming to get me. See my knees are hunched, knuckles
tight. I am poised, ready and waiting for them. I will spit in
their eye. The birds will plop their droppings on their heads.
The branches of the trees will flay them alive. For no one can
touch me. Mama is gone away. A blue apron where I put my
head, smelling crisp and fresh. Grandad says she is sick. Sick
is the blister on my thumb. I am sick too but I didn't leave
her. Mama is screaming now. Screaming! Across from me are
tall hedges. Under me is a bed of white flowers. I make a
chain with the flowers and wear it around my neck. From the
front of Grandad's house I can see a hill. He says the fairies
live there. Now I talk to the fairies with my chain around my
neck. Then I gather the daisy chain into a bundle with my
fist and break the circle. I see a clump of primroses growing
in the middle of the grass. I push my nose into the yellow
cups and kiss each one to make them grow. "Grow, grow, my
little beauties."

I am tired of sitting under this apple tree now. I will
become a race horse. Silky smooth. Black as the coal
Grandad keeps in the pigsty. Over the tall hedges I gracefully
glide. Panting, I stop only to gather speed. Then down to the
bottom of the orchard where I trot around proudly, my head
back and my neck arched to gather speed again. I gallop,
flying through the orchard. My hooves scatter the earth. Up
and over the strawberry plants. This is my new home.
Grandad says I can stay forever. So I will. I will be the green-
fly on the roses. I will stick to the base of the leaves and suck
the juicy fruits until I am fat and contented. Then I will
sleep while the autumn comes and the flowers die. The trees
will be bare, distraught from the tiresome winds and heavy
rains. I will sleep until I'm dead like my Mama.

There was another house somewhere, with ceilings as high
as the sky and green-painted walls so distant. I lie in a bed
under strange blankets and pull them over my head. A figure
looms over and says, "You are in a home now. You'll be stay-
ing here until your mother gets better." In the middle of the

ocean I row my boat with my fingers. My fingers are all cold and icy but I have lost my oars. The water caresses the side of the boat like a hungry tongue. Soon I will be sitting on the bottom of the ocean crying, "Mama! Where are you?" And she will not hear me because my mouth will be full of water. Bubbles will float like notes of music from my lips. I cannot breathe as I sit here on the bottom of the ocean.

I hang onto the bedclothes with my fists and the voice above scolds me. Does she not know I'm not here? I'm in the jungle surrounded by trees and bushes. I am so hungry and thirsty. The sun beats me with its heat like a whip. But in the distance I can see my Mama. I run and stumble and fall over hidden rocks. When I look up again she is gone. I walk and walk until again in the distance I can see her. But she cannot see me. I wave my hands in the air as she looks far beyond where I stand. I whimper and whimper calling to her. "Remember me. Remember me." When she hears me she starts to run. Away, until she becomes just a whiff of wind. I am screaming! Screaming!

At the end of the town a side road led up to the cemetery. Everyone got out to walk the rest of the way. The air was cold and damp. Four men carried the coffin on their shoulders through the graveyard. They placed it on four planks over the freshly dug grave. People stood around in small groups. Watchful hungry eyes anxious to witness the final moment. His last drop of blood a reminder of their own. The priest stood at the top of the grave. He turned his coat collar up before opening a prayer book. "Out of the depths we have cried onto Thee, O lord," he prayed.

You lay there so still, so unlike you. There was only you and I. Let me hear your laughter, now. Mine is inside tinkling, tinkling. What was love, Father? Love was your hands on me. Not the Big Dark but you, you red-faced cur, coming into the room. You stood over by the wall where I could see the check shirt through the light of the window. And Sara said, "What are you lookin' at me like that for? Maggie, he's going to kill me." Only I knew you weren't, not the way she meant, because I had been on the wall watching for eight years. Eight years, yes long enough to know what you had done to Esther and that you would do the same to me. I knew you would when I looked down and saw the soft pink between my legs and said, "Yes. That is soft and dewy. That is my pleasure." I knew you would come and take it away from me. So you stood by the side of the bed and then you were on top of me crushing me down. You pulled back the blankets and stretched my hands out either side of me so I couldn't move. I died then. I felt nothing except the emptiness of Night's City.

When you were gone Sara went downstairs. Esther was reading the paper. Sara drank a glass of water and I watched Esther, waited for her to say, "It is sometimes that terrible." But she stared over for one minute or less and in that time I knew that she knew and I could drown in my own blood because she had to drown in hers. "I hate myself," I said. "Hate, hate, hate, myself." But Sara would not believe me. She just would not. For weeks afterwards she screamed through the nights so they took her away to hospital to forget what they wanted me to forget. But I did not.

One day I spat on the ground outside our gate. A venomous spit from my mouth to the ground. The spittle lay there with no design or shape. A greeny yellow mucus. I was mucus. The next day I ran out to see if the spittle was still there. Someone had walked on it. It was buried in the sole of someone's shoe.

Come with me to the valley of silence. "You're a queer one," Esther said. "What are you staring out through the curtains for? Well? What are you looking at, Sara?" But Sara didn't know. I saw; all withered ashes floating on the wind. All skin-a-burning. All breasts a-sagging. All legs a-dragging. Veins protruding. Faces fading, shoulders aching, bodies breaking, wind a-howling, rain a-crying, night-time falling, daytime dawning, colours changing, the earth a-crumbling, women dying, their tongues unmoving, their spirits flagging all over the seed of sons.

It began to rain heavily. People huddled closer to the grave, the prayers coming louder from their mouths as they tried to

drown out the wind and rain. There were fifty or more at
the funeral. Fifty bedraggled clowns. I wanted to scream into
the crowd, "Go away, fools. Do you not see we are holding
a carnival here. Do not stand there with your sullen faces.
Smile and dance and play to the music that floats over your
heads. And Esther, you rhyme off nonsensical sympathies
to her and all you do is disturb her roaming thoughts. She is
searching the house from top-to-bottom in her head looking
for the insurance policy. For who else will pay for this
grand affair?"

Oh! Mother, Mother. Where were you? On your knees or
in the loo? Oh God, I had dreams! Hold me to your breast, O
Mother. Remember I am yours. You used to touch me, hug
me, hold me close; but only if I was a good girl and said
over and over again, "I hate men. I hate men." "Remember
this," I whispered to Sara. "Remember this. All men are
bastards."

I watch the dusk settle on the ceiling and move down the
walls inch-by-inch until it reaches the skirting board and the
last glow of dusk spreads like a shallow tide in the centre of
the floor. I lie waiting for the City of Night to fall. Bodies
become humps and ridges invading the quiet night like circus
clowns. Their voices become a single whisper, the last whim-
pering cry between sound and silence. Humans appear,
some squatting down in the shadows while others edge their
way along the narrow streets. In the centre of the City there
is a street which is different from the others. An angular
street lamp stands at the end of it, throwing off an eerie
beam. Out of the darkness steps a woman. She walks down
the street and stands waiting under the lamp. A whisper
comes, one that I heard often in Night's City. It floats
through the darkness, a high pitched whisper, "We can't
because of Sara," it says. But I am already waiting in the
City. It's too late now.

The woman turns slightly as the whisper floats from wall
to wall. It sidles in and out of the shadows as though anxious
that the whole City should hear it. Then it floats up the
street towards the woman. Only then do I see the difference

between this street and the others. The walls on either side are made of sponge. The road is slightly oval like a long curved passageway. A brownish mucus covers it. The bloodless mouth and the tomb-like eyes of the woman watch a man standing at the bottom of the street. She beckons to him and the pink sponge walls suck slowly in and out. He steps quite assertively, though somewhat clumsily, into the street. As he walks up towards her the movements of the walls grow stronger and he is flung from side to side like a bouncing ball. In the midst of this I see another figure towering over a woman. The figure has encased the body beneath him and I can hear his heavy breathing as he bends down towards her. She turns her face away from him. I leap into the darkness towards the large body. He turns in anger and moves in my direction. Then I see the man in Night's City bouncing from wall to wall. At last he reaches the woman under the street lamp. She smiles at him as the foam-like walls start to close in around him, squeezing him to death. The woman's eyes are fixed on him like two windows peering into a graveyard.

The carnival was over. I walked through the streets of the town and when I reached the seafront I walked out onto the beach. The sand was still damp from the outgoing tide. The moon cast silvery streaks over the waves like pathways. Watching the movements of the water I wondered what it would be like to walk on the waves and feel the palmy shapes beneath my feet. Soothing to think of wetness on lips and the salty water filling my lungs. Then to disappear forever under the great bed of weaving darkness. I cupped my hands either side of my mouth and the words were almost drowned in the roaring of the sea. So that they came as a whisper and I wondered again why I should repeatedly call to myself.

SARA

"My Ma was a good woman. Da beat us sometimes but that's because we were bad. He loved us all the same. And my Ma loved me. My Ma LOVED ME. Someday I'll get married and have children just like she did. Everything will be all right then. I don't hate being a woman. I don't. I don't."

SELECTED DALKEY ARCHIVE PAPERBACKS

FOR A FULL LIST OF PUBLICATIONS, VISIT:
www.dalkeyarchive.com

SELECTED DALKEY ARCHIVE PAPERBACKS

FOR A FULL LIST OF PUBLICATIONS, VISIT:
www.dalkeyarchive.com